THE TURKEY KILLER

THE TURKEY
KILLER

JACK SNOW

THE TURKEY KILLER
JACK SNOW

ISBN: 978-1-943927-36-4

CONTENTS

DEDICATION

To my wife Bonne, who encourages and supports me in all
my life endeavors, I dedicate this novel.

In memory

In memory of Yeoman Smith, who was just as I describe in the book. Yeoman was the greatest of friends, storytellers, neighbors, and hunting buddies.

We all miss him at The Shed.

PROLOGUE

Few people come to visit anymore. Oh, occasionally, a lost carful of kids looking for the amusement park and sometimes one of my daughters or grandchildren will stop by for a short visit. But Bonnie and I do just fine living off the side of this old mountain overlooking Blowing Rock, North Carolina. Now in our early seventies, we have resigned ourselves to a simpler life and a simpler existence. I haven't hunted since the tragedy, and I don't even have the desire to wet a fishing hook. Bonnie and I just want to live the remainder of our days left alone. Lots of nights, we find ourselves quietly rocking on this old front porch, listening to the mountains. I never knew that mountains could communicate with one's soul, but this old Blue Ridge mountain has done wonders to help me forget. Many nights, I get lost in the mountain's winds, letting them carry me back to our old home, to a better time when our friends were close and our family even closer.

But not this particular day because we had a visitor who brought back all the bad memories Bonnie and I thought we had left back in Davie County. This morning, just after a country breakfast, I got up from the table as usual and emptied the scraps of country ham, eggs, and grits from my plate back into the skillet. I knew that my old bird dog, Sadie, was ready to eat her morning's due. Sadie, her hunting spirit broken like mine, was now retired and resigned to living the rest of her days in whatever peace came her way. As I opened the screen door on the back porch, headed for Sadie's dog pen, I heard the familiar sound of a lost car slowly approaching this old cabin. Our gravel road has a sound of its own. The rocks disheveled by the automobile gave me a sense of neither fright nor calm, but one of anticipation of who was disturbing my world, and for what reason. As the new, shiny car rolled to a stop, I strolled from the backyard around to the front porch to greet this lost tourist.

Just as I reached the front yard, the car door slowly opened, and a pudgy, overweight young man emerged. The first things I noticed, other than his size, were a flashy earring and baggy, drooping jeans. *Another lost kid looking for the amusement park has gotten off the main highway and onto my long dirt driveway and right into my world*, I thought.

"Go back the way you came. It's two miles to the hard-surface road. Take a left, then go exactly 2.8 miles and turn left on Highway 421. The amusement park is on the right," I said.

The young man looked deep into my eyes and asked, "Is your name Rumsey, Jack Rumsey?"

A sense of fear, almost a sickening feeling, ran through my body, and I was just barely able to get the words out. "Who wants to know?" I said.

"My name is Cannon Swain, and I live in Mocksville," he softly said. After a few seconds of silence, he added, "And if you're Jack Rumsey, I've been looking for you for over a year now."

Turning my back to him, I said more forcibly, "Yeah, I'm Jack Rumsey, and I don't know any Swains, so kindly turn your damn car around and leave me be."

"My grandpa was Yeoman Swain, and I need you to help me understand about him," he said.

My body froze, just like when, as a kid, I jumped into the creek after getting up hay all day in August. To keep from falling down, I stepped onto the front porch to sit and take a closer look at this young man. "That was years ago, a time I have forgotten and do not wish to remember, so just get back in your car and leave me be," I said.

The young man just stared into my eyes once more and quietly said, "May I just sit with you awhile?"

My mind, body, and soul wanted to say no, but to my horror I simply waved for him to sit in Bonnie's rocking chair.

This young man was all of only five-foot-two and must have weighed at least 275 pounds. He had sandy brown hair, blue eyes, a baby face, and a real white complexion and was the spitting image of a young friend long forgotten. When Cannon began to step onto the porch, his big foot slipped on the old granite rock used for a step, and he must have fallen for what seemed like minutes. When he finally landed, I couldn't help laughing out loud at the sight, just as I would have if it had been my old friend Yeoman himself.

As I jumped from my rocking chair to help him up, Bonnie came through the house, opened the screen door, and hollered, "What's going on? Who are you, and what are you doing here?"

"Bonnie," I said, "this clumsy young man is Cannon Swain, and he just stopped by to talk."

"Well, you can talk all you want, but we are not buying anything, and besides, you don't need to be wasting time talking. You and I both have a garden to tend to," she snapped.

I looked over at Bonnie as I finished helping Cannon to her chair. "This is Yeoman Swain's grandson," I explained. Excited fear flashed in my wife's eyes as she grabbed my arm in concern. I pulled her close to me and said reassuringly, "It's okay, dear. Let's just listen to what he has to say, and then we'll send him on his way. If he's anything like Yeoman, now that he's found us, if we don't listen, he'll just keep coming back and bothering us."

"Well, he's not sitting in my rocking chair. As young as he is, let him sit in the straight-back chair," Bonnie said, trying to sound more courageous.

As Bonnie and I sat in our rocking chairs, a warm, gentle spring breeze rustled through the leaves of the poplar trees almost on cue to calm our nerves. We didn't know what this young man had to say, or what information he wanted, but for some reason we just knew he meant us no harm.

I detected a quiver in his chubby chin and his voice as he began to speak. "My name is Cannon Swain, and I live by myself in Mocksville. My parents died in a car crash when I was eight, and I was sent to live with foster parents until I graduated from high school, just a little over two years ago. When I graduated, not having any family, and with nowhere to go, it was an easy decision for me to try to join the army. That's why I'm here."

"Wait a minute, son. I can't help you get into the army. I don't have any connections there or even know anyone in the army," I tried to explain.

"No, no, you don't understand. I'm not here for that. I'm here to learn about my grandfather," he softly said. "You see, when I went for my physical to get into the army, they found that, well, I'm dying. I have untreatable cancer and have only approximately nine months to live."

What do you say when someone, especially someone you don't know, tells you he's dying? I slowly rose to my feet and walked over to the young man. "I'm sorry to hear your sad news, but I don't see how I can help. So, if you'll excuse me, my wife and I have to work in the garden," I said, looking into his troubled eyes.

"I just want to know what really happened to my grandpa before I die. I've asked all over the county and spoken to everyone I can find who knew my grandpa, about his death. The answer I always get is that only Jack Rumsey knows what really happened to Yeoman. That's exactly why I'm here," he calmly said.

Nothing but silence was left among the three of us on the porch. Bonnie and I now knew why this young stranger had tracked me down.

Bonnie was the first to move. Rising from her rocking chair, she slowly strolled by and bent to whisper in my ear, "You owe this man an answer."

I whispered back, "I owe this man nothing. I'm sorry for his illness, but I owe him nothing. I'm just trying to forget."

Bonnie then smiled, gently held my hand in hers, looked at the sick young man, and said aloud, "Then you owe it to your close friend Yeoman." She then turned, opened the screen door, and retired into the old log house.

The two of us must have sat there on the porch for only a few minutes, but it seemed like hours. My mind flashed back to happier times, when Bonnie and I lived on our small farm and I used to hunt, fish, and sit around campfires with Yeoman and other friends. We would sit for hours eating, drinking, and telling hunting and fishing lies. During those simple times, my friends and I had developed bonds and lasting friendships that I thought even death would not destroy.

Not realizing my head was bowed, I slowly raised my tear-filled eyes to find this young man staring at me, waiting for an answer.

I barely whispered, "If I tell you the real story of your grandfather, will you then go and leave me in peace?"

He simply nodded.

"Well, Cannon, where do I start? Guess I'll just start from the time in Davie County when Bonnie and I were the happiest."

CHAPTER ONE

It was a cool, brisk November day, and the leaves were flying off the trees by the thousands. Half asleep sitting in my easy chair just under the front porch of my new garage, I was fully awakened when a damp, cold, wet rag hit me directly in the face.

"Thought you were cooking hamburgers for your hunting buddies today," my wife said, giggling about the wet rag. Bonnie and I had been married for thirty-three years then, and I've said many times that if God actually put angels on this earth, I was lucky enough to marry one. She was a beautiful woman who had not been damaged by the years or the tough times we endured making a living or the pleasures of raising three lovely daughters.

"I'm getting up," I said. "Besides, I've got plenty of time."

"No, you don't. You haven't even swept your hunting garage," Bonnie said.

I had always wanted a combination garage and hunting, fishing, and party shed, and in April, on my fifty-second birthday, Bonnie had hired my friend Larry Wyatt to build my dream. "The Shed," the likes of which no sportsman in Davie County, North Carolina, had ever seen, was absolutely the perfect hangout for me and my hunting buddies. The Shed was thirty by thirty-six feet and two stories, with a huge front porch, lots of ceiling fans, inside cedar paneling, a manly bathroom, a gun safe, a refrigerator full of beer, concrete stained floors, a full kitchen, a wood heating stove, and lots and lots of tools. I even had tools to fix other tools in my perfect, man's dream hunting and party shed.

"Screw the cleaning. The guys only care about beer, food, and telling stories. We're probably going to eat outside anyway," I added, trying to keep from doing any work.

"Suit yourself. I could care less about your mesquite

pit-cooked hamburgers and your hunting lies anyway," Bonnie said.

"Then shut up and get yourself back in the house, but give me a kiss before you leave," I said. She and I both knew I was just kidding about the shutting up part, but I was serious about the kiss. It was just my luck she turned and went strolling across the yard and into the house.

I had invited the local hunting guys over for hamburgers cooked over a fire pit of mesquite wood. In North Carolina, mesquite wood cooking is a delightful experience. Mesquite is a small bush or tree almost black in color, found mostly in southwest Texas. This wood burns extremely hot and creates an aroma and flavor all its own. In fact, mesquite wood chips sold in local stores are very expensive. This particular mesquite wood was shipped to me by my friend Blaine Thomas. Blaine was born and raised in Laredo, Texas, a cow town about thirty miles north of Mexico. Blaine had gotten out of the cow business and was now in the hunting and fishing business. During hunting season, he made a good living leasing ranches and selling south Texas deer hunts to people just like me. In the off-season, he guided saltwater trout-fishing excursions in the Baytown area. Blaine was a good guy, a good friend, and a halfway decent guide.

Slowly but surely, the guys began to show up, looking for cold beer and something to snack on while the burgers cooked and the hunting lies flew. First to arrive was Larry Wyatt, a local builder well known and respected throughout the county. The most famous work of Larry's was The Shed, or at least the most famous to me. Larry was a tall, lanky man who laughed more than he talked and had never met a stranger. Larry was respected by his peers as a good sportsman and avid deer hunter. Next to arrive were my two next-door neighbors, Delmar Haines and Buford Wilson. Delmar and Buford were also the best of friends, even though Buford was Delmar's brother-in-law. Both were avid deer hunters. Neither Delmar, Buford, nor Larry were good wing shooters or cared much about any other type of hunting or fishing. JP, Delmar Haines's son, was the next to arrive. JP, a big country boy with a six-pack appreciation, came riding up to The Shed on his new 650 Arctic Cat ATV.

"Can't ride this and dip Copenhagen, too," mumbled JP through a half-hardy grin.

"Why not?" asked Buford.

"Goes so fast, spits the shit in my eyes," JP answered.

JP was the only man I knew below thirty-five years old who had a short flat-top haircut. I probably would not call JP a Davie County redneck, but he was as close to it as I guess I was. He and I had begun hunting and fishing together about six years earlier. In that time, I watched JP mature into a fine young man. He was honest, hardworking, and above all a loyal friend.

We were all standing around the fire pit and admiring JP's new ATV when Buford asked, "Where's Mike and Brian?"

Before anyone could answer, Delmar added, "And Yeoman. I've never known Yeoman to miss any meals."

"I'll have you know, I've lost fifty pounds on the Atkins Diet," Yeoman yelled from The Shed. "All I eat is dadgum chicken, though. Every meal, chicken, chicken, chicken. Why, I've ate so much chicken, I wake up in the mornings with the taste of wet feathers in my mouth."

Everyone around the pit roared with laughter.

Yeoman was as well known throughout the county as any man. You just couldn't help liking Yeoman. He weighed close to 350 pounds, was about five-foot-four, and always had a dip of tobacco in his mouth and a smile on his face. He was almost like a modern-day Santa Claus with his kindness for people, especially children. He knew everyone in Davie, their mothers and fathers, and probably a story about their families. I suspected that many of the stories Yeoman told, if not all of them, stretched the truth a lot, but no one in our hunting group ever got tired of hearing them.

I first met Yeoman many years ago. I was new to Davie County, and just on a whim I decided to run for county commissioner. Yeoman was campaign manager for his longtime friend Layne Watson. Layne, like Yeoman, was well known throughout the county. Layne was campaigning for commissioner because of his love for the land, its country nature, and the people who lived and worked there every day. Yeoman did a great job as campaign manager, and he and his candidate beat me by a landslide. My total campaign was giving out pens, cups, and chewing tobacco at Andy's Country Store. Andy's was where all the local farmers and just good old country boys hung out drinking Cokes, telling lies, chewing tobacco, and huddling around the wood stove.

These things passed the time for a lot of my friends. When everyone gathered around the wood stove, I would seize the opportunity to ask for their votes for commissioner.

One day while I was trying to drum up a few votes, Yeoman cut my speech short by interrupting. "You don't stand a chance, young man." Yeoman made sure he spoke loud enough for the entire crowd of Coke drinkers to hear. "We don't know you, and us folks around this county don't cotton to outsiders trying to come here and run things."

It was true that my wife and I had recently bought forty-three acres in Davie when we moved from neighboring Forsyth County.

"It's true you and Layne will probably beat me like a borrowed mule, but I'll still be in the hunt. Yeoman, I know I'll get at least four votes come Election Day," I said, waiting for him to fall into the trap I had just laid.

Yeoman took off his sweat-rimmed ball cap and said, "Wait a darn minute. You and your wife and three daughters can vote. To my count, that adds up to five."

"Don't think my youngest daughter, Kathy, is going to vote for me," I answered.

Everyone around the wood stove either roared with laughter or was trying to laugh but was choking on Coke and chewing tobacco.

Every day, Yeoman and I replayed this routine. And every day, I would answer the same. Yeoman would wheeze with laughter, slap me on the back, and say, "For someone from Forsyth County, Rumsey, you're all right, but we'll still whip you on Election Day."

Election Day came and went, and they did beat me, but I really was the winner because I had a new great friend in Yeoman Swain.

Yeoman liked to hunt almost as much as anyone in our group. He hunted deer, turkeys, doves, rabbits, squirrels, and any other animals that were legal to shoot.

Delmar grabbed the shovel and began to spread the hot mesquite coals in the fire pit. "This fire looks ready to me," he said.

Buford said, "Then reckon I ought to get the grill top so we can get this party started."

Buford and I walked down to the pole barn, where the grill top hung from a sixteen-penny nail driven into the main beam of the barn. The pole barn was twenty feet deep and thirty feet wide, with an open front and six-inch boards down both sides and the back. The poles that supported the barn and the roof were made of treated six-by-six-inch lumber, braced by treated two-by-four-inch crossbars. The roof was red metal attached by one-inch screws placed about every two feet across each section. Buford and Delmar, along with me, JP, and Don and Matt Markland, helped build this barn just before deer season. We built it approximately a hundred yards from The Shed, and I used it to store a Kubota tractor, an Arctic Cat ATV, a Turf Tiger commercial lawn mower, and lawn mower attachments. One thing was for sure—that pole barn would be standing long after I was gone.

"The old barn looks good, even though you and Delmar built it," said Buford.

"What do you mean, me and Delmar? You and Delmar were the ones that really built this thing. JP, Don, Matt, and I just carried boards and beer to you two. I can't build nothing, fix nothing, or paint nothing. Thank goodness God gave me a mouth, because if I couldn't sell, me and Bonnie would starve to death," I said.

"You're right. You are the best salesperson I've ever met. I bet you could sell used underwear back to Hanes. Me, I couldn't sell a whore in a lumber camp, so I have to be good with my hands. Hard work is my life," Buford explained with a grin on his face.

"Are you going to grab the other side of this grill, or are we going to stay down here and jaw all night?" I asked.

As we carried the grill top back to the pit, it was evident that Mike and Brian had arrived. Brian had already jumped on JP's new ATV and was cutting donuts in the pasture beside The Shed.

"He's going to kill himself one of these days," Buford said.

When he was a kid, Brian used to race dirt bikes all around the county. He had broken about every bone in his body, and his shoulder blade at least three times. I don't guess he ever figured out that maybe he was just not built to ride those things. Brian had to be pushing seven feet tall. He was long and lanky and thin as a rail. Brian was Larry Wyatt's youngest son and had exactly the same personality as Larry. Brian, who had recently married, lived about two miles from me and had a real nice piece of land with a single-wide mobile home. He was a true Davie County redneck who once got struck by lightning while holding on to a CB antenna. All this boy knew was work. Right out of high school, Brian went to work grading and hauling for the local builders. He once told me that besides hunting and fishing, work was his favorite pastime. I had hunted and fished with Brian for many years and found him to be a real sportsman. He was always ready to hunt and did so with the passion and zeal of a fourteen-year-old kid. Brian loved hunting all kinds of game, including quail and ducks, but deer hunting was his passion.

I saw that Mike had found the washtub filled with beer and ice and had already cracked the top on one and was looking for the pre-dinner snacks.

"Where are your famous Redneck Caviar and chips?" Mike asked.

"In the refrigerator!" I yelled as Buford and I placed the grill on the pit of hot mesquite coals. Everyone loved my Redneck Caviar.

"What's in that stuff, anyway?" Buford asked.

"Well, it's simple. You just combine two cans of black-eyed peas, two cans of shoepeg corn, two cans of Rotel tomatoes, one green pepper, diced, one red pepper, diced, a dozen small green onions, chopped, and a bottle of Italian dressing. Chill for one hour and serve with tortilla chips," I replied. It was a great recipe that hit the spot with hunters, buddies, and fellow beer drinkers.

I lost sight of Mike when he headed for the refrigerator, followed very closely by Yeoman. I'd known Mike Dillion since I was just three years old. His uncle Charles was the meanest and roughest man in Forsyth County, and was married to my aunt on my mother's side. So he and I kind of grew up together, went to school together, played football and baseball together, but most of all hunted and fished together. Mike was just a couple of years older than I, and we had about the same build and weight. He was about five-foot-nine and weighed about 175 pounds. He had black hair and a friendly personality. Several years ago, Mike bought a farm just down the road from my place. His farm was absolutely beautiful. It had approximately eighty-two acres, with a real nice brick home overlooking a five-acre lake. His lake had tons of three-to ten-pound bass and plenty of channel catfish and bream. Many nights, Mike, JP, and I fished, drank beer, and fried catfish until the wee hours of the morning.

Yeoman was the first to break the silence after Buford and I positioned the grill top just right over the coals. "When are we going to eat?" he asked.

"Is that all you think about, Yeoman? 'Sides, you've got a big bowl of Redneck Caviar and chips," Delmar joked.

Before Yeoman could answer, Brian slid the Arctic Cat to a stop, jumped off, and said, "Yeoman, I thought you and Dr. Atkins were on a diet."

Yeoman looked puzzled about whom to answer first, and just simply looked at me and said, "Are you going to cook burgers or not?" He then turned to Brian and Delmar and said, "Look, let's get off the diet stuff, okay? I used to have to pull my britches down just to put my hands in my pockets, but now with Dr. Atkins's help, I can do that standing or sitting, thank you very much."

JP interrupted as he came from the kitchen of The Shed, headed toward the fire pit with a huge tray of burgers that appeared to be about a pound apiece. "Get out of the way,

Yo-Man. These burgers are heavy," JP announced in an annoying voice.

"Man, these are going to be good. One cup of water per pound of burger, and with all the seasonings I added, these will melt in your mouth," I said.

"Dr. Atkins said I can have all the beef I want, so I think I'll have three or four burgers before I try to figure out what to eat for dessert," Yeoman announced.

"Hey, I bet if we were to take your blood type right now, it would be Rocky Road," JP joked.

"I thought we said no more diet jokes," Yeoman snapped back.

"You're the one that keeps talking about Dr. Atkins," JP said in self-defense.

Both were interrupted when the first burger hit the grill with a sizzling sound and an aroma that separated the two friends. Yeoman then turned and went back into The Shed.

JP pulled up a white plastic lawn chair next to the pit and announced, "Hey, Yo-Man, since you're up, when you come back, bring us a beer."

Big, tall Brian strolled up to help me place the remaining

morsels of meat on the grill and said, "I never get tired of eating mesquite-cooked meat. Sure beats our hickory wood we normally cook with."

Yeoman, looking for sympathy, said, "Brian, tell JP and Delmar to get off the fat jokes, would you?"

"No problem, Yeoman. I'll just hit JP on top of the head so hard it will sprain his ankles," Brian said.

Brian was so much taller than anyone else at The Shed, he probably could have done just that. These were the reasons we gathered at The Shed in the first place—cooking meat, snacking on Redneck Caviar, telling jokes and hunting and fishing stories, and drinking beer.

"Do you think we'll have good food in Texas when we go deer hunting in January?" Yeoman asked.

JP quickly answered, "The cook, Mr. Roy, used to be Queen Elizabeth's and Princess Diana's Mexican cook, or so they say. It says on their website that Mr. Roy cooks brisket with every meal."

"Well, if that's true, then it's no wonder Princess Diana was so skinny. She must have always had the squirts from all the brisket Mr. Roy cooked for breakfast, lunch, and dinner,"

Brian said.

We ate every hamburger, along with all the Redneck Caviar. We were just about to open a second case of beer when JP yelled, "I need help cleaning up the dishes! Don't everyone jump up at one time." JP opened a fresh Miller Lite, left the kitchen, and pulled up a chair around the fire pit. "Let's talk about January's deer hunt. I didn't want to fool with the damn dishes anyway. I was just trying to be neighborly."

Everyone grabbed the white plastic chairs Bonnie had bought from Walmart and sat around the same fire pit that just cooked forty-two huge hamburgers.

"All right, here's the deal. I'm going to shoot the biggest buck that has ever been shot in the state of Texas," Yeoman explained.

"Yeoman, if you saw the biggest buck in Texas, you'd just wet your pants," Brian chuckled.

"Yeah, right. When it comes to deer hunting, I'm the toughest, most vicious hunter alive," said Yeoman. "Why, I've even killed a deer with my bare hands and a knife."

Everyone around the fire laughed uncontrollably.

Yeoman, now with a red face, said, "Let me tell you the story before you guys bust a gut."

"Please do, Yo-Man. But before you do, let me get a fresh beer. All right, everyone, quiet down and let's listen to the great hunter," I said, opening my last beer of the evening.

"I was hunting down off Highway 64, right at the river that separates Davie County and Davidson County," Yeoman explained. "There were about 650 acres of prime deer hunting that had lots of tall, big oak trees to put stands in."

"Like you could get your big butt in a tree stand," laughed JP.

"Hey, this was about thirty years and 150 pounds ago, JP," snapped Yeoman. "Well, anyway, as I was saying, I was hunting out of a stand in a tall white oak tree when, all of a sudden, a pain hit me. I had to pee and pee right then. So I quickly climbed out of my stand with my gun over my shoulder, and to the bottom of the tree I went. Just as soon as I hit the ground and started peeing, I heard a limb crack about fifty yards behind me, toward the river."

Everyone was on the edge of their seats, waiting for Yeoman to get to what we thought was the punch line.

"It was a deer, a buck, that looked to be an eight-pointer," explained Yeoman. "I slowly raised my gun and shot this deer just behind the shoulder, where I knew that it would be a quick kill. After I shot, the deer kicked up his back legs and ran out of sight over the hill toward the river bottom. When I finished peeing, it began to rain a hard and steady cold rain."

"You said you killed the deer with your knife. I knew this was just another one of your stories," interrupted Brian.

"If you'll shut up, I'll finish telling you the rest of the hunt, Brian," said Yeoman. "I leaned my gun on the oak tree and went looking for the buck's blood trail. First, there was a lot of blood and he was easy to trail, but then as it rained harder the trail went away, so I was just blindly looking for what I knew had to be a dead deer by now. Then, all of a sudden, I saw the buck lying in a thicket with his head slightly raised. *Not quite dead yet*, I thought. Figuring it was almost dead, I thought I would just sneak up behind the deer, jump on his back, and slit his throat."

Now, everyone was laughing, just imagining Yeoman on the back of a wounded, yet alive, buck.

"The plan was working perfectly, and I slipped through

the wet leaves within two feet of this wounded deer. Then I pounced like a wild man onto this deer's back with my knife ready to strike, when, all of a sudden, he jumped up and started running around in circles with me on his back." Yeoman spoke more excitedly now. "This deer, with me on his back, ran through every thicket and briar patch on the river bottom. I stabbed that deer while I was getting the hell beat out of me by trees and briars. Finally, victory. The deer slowly lay down and died in the muddy river bottom with me still on his back. My deer and I just lay there while I tried my best to breathe and recover from the worst beating of my life. The rain was coming down harder when I wrapped my belt around the buck's antlers for the long drag out of the woods and into the back of my truck. Now, here's the best part. As I was dragging that deer out of the woods, I saw another buck lying at the edge of a pine thicket. As I got closer, I realized that this second deer was actually the one I shot, and the one I was dragging was not wounded at all."

Brian spit beer into the fire to keep from choking, and Mike and the rest of the guys cracked up. Yeoman knew he had suckered us and laughed uncontrollably. All of a sudden, we heard a loud crack. Pieces of white plastic chair went flying through the air, and Yeoman's head just missed the front of the tractor as he hit the ground and rolled down the hill by the fire pit. Everyone ran to Yeoman's side to make sure he was okay. We gathered around and helped him up.

Yeoman was still laughing when he got to his feet, announced to everyone he was okay, and said, "What a great way to end the night."

I agreed, as we were all out of beer anyway.

As all my hunting buddies and I slowly staggered to The Shed, Delmar said, "Damn, Yo-Man, when I saw all this plastic flying, I just knew you'd be farting milk jugs for the next couple of weeks. Glad you're okay, buddy."

Chapter Two

The guys and I got together quite a bit throughout the long winter as we waited patiently on our upcoming Texas deer hunt. Soon, it was the night before leaving for the long-awaited trip. Bonnie, as always, helped me pack my suitcase and felt sad that I was leaving.

"Make sure you pack your long handles and plenty of clean underwear," she said. "You already know from their website that they will be cooking brisket with every meal, and you know how you'll have trouble with all the fat."

"Bonnie, the average temperature in Laredo is about seventy-five, so I won't need any long underwear, and I plan not to eat any of Mr. Roy's brisket," I said. "Look at the bottom of my suitcase and you'll see I'm prepared to eat well and not get diarrhea."

Bonnie dug down deep in my hunting suitcase and found my stash of twenty-four cans of Beanee Weenee, twelve cans of Treet meat, and a box of saltine crackers.

"Looks like it will be a noisy time in the bunkhouse," Bonnie said.

"Yeah, with my beans and Yeoman's snoring, it should be a hoot, no pun intended," I said.

Just then, the phone rang, and it was Yeoman on the line. This was Yeoman's first time hunting in Texas, and he was extremely excited.

"Hello, Yeoman, are you ready to go?" I asked.

"I've been packed and ready for the last three days," Yeoman said. The only thing he dreaded was the flight. "You know, those small fifty-passenger jets have no room for a full-figured guy like me."

"Oh, no, Yeoman, we're flying from Greensboro to Corpus on a 737, and we're flying first class," I said. "There's no need to worry about your size because you'll be flying with me in the front of the plane."

"Man, that's a relief, but I'm still afraid of flying. If we were meant to fly, God would have given us wings," said Yeoman.

"Yeoman, it's nothing to fly. I fly over twenty thousand miles a year," I said, trying to comfort my friend. "Just have you a short Jack Daniel's when you get on the plane, and you'll go to sleep before it ever leaves the ground. That way, you won't even know you're flying, and I'll wake you up in Corpus." I was barely able to hold my laughter. I planned to give Yeoman not only the best hunting trip but also the most eventful flight, one that he and my buddies would not soon forget. "I'll pick you up at five-thirty in the morning. Don't oversleep," I said.

"No sleeping for me tonight. See you at five-thirty. Good night," said Yeoman.

When I hung up the phone, Bonnie just looked at me and said, "You better not scare Yeoman on that plane. What if he has a heart attack?"

I said, "Now, Bonnie, you know I'm just going to give Yeoman and the guys something to talk about. And besides,

Yeoman won't be scared unless he really goes to sleep on the plane."

At five on Sunday morning, JP blew the horn of his Ford pickup. I opened the front door as the blast from the horn got louder and louder. Quickly, I flicked the switch of the lamppost light to let JP know I was up, and to quit blowing that obnoxious horn.

Bonnie was standing in the facing of the front door as I gathered up my hunting gear. "Have fun, be safe, and remember that I love you," she said with just a touch of a whine in her voice. Bonnie had always hated to see me leave ever since we were married. But as much as I had to travel for our business and for the love of hunting and fishing, I thought she would have gotten used to it by then.

"Don't worry. I'll be fine," I said.

"I just really hate to see you go," Bonnie explained.

"Give me a kiss goodbye, and I'll call you tonight," I said, trying to reassure her that I would be okay.

"And tell JP, the next time he blows that horn in my driveway, I'm going to skin his head," Bonnie said, trying to act angry.

"Can't. It's already been skinned. Look at his new flat-top haircut," I said, laughing.

"Get on out of here. I love you. Call me," Bonnie said as she pushed the door wider, enabling me to get more gear out and onto the front porch.

There sat JP in his new white Ford F-150 four-door pickup, looking as if he had done nothing wrong, especially anything involving a horn.

"Come help me with this stuff!" I yelled to JP.

Slowly, the door of the truck swung open, and out rolled JP. "No problem," he said, grabbing up hunting bags and guns as he strolled down the sidewalk.

I turned and saw Bonnie standing on the front porch. "We're off to the South Texas Hilton. I'll call you when we get there. I love you," I yelled to Bonnie when I climbed into the front seat of the truck.

JP loaded the last bag, jumped into the driver's side, and blinked the headlights to tell Miss Bonnie goodbye. In just a few seconds, my house was out of sight and we were on our way down Howardtown Road to pick up Brian, then Yeoman.

"Man, I've been looking forward to this deer-hunting trip since fall," I said to JP.

"Yeah, me, too. I hope the deer hunting is better in Texas than here in North Carolina," JP responded.

"Forget the deer hunting, I just hope I can eat the food," I said.

"Don't matter to me none about the food because I brought two whole boxes of ammonia," explained JP.

"Ammonia? Oh, you mean Imodium," I said.

"Oh yeah, I mean Imodium. I guess if it was ammonia, I'd be farting soap bubbles," JP said while laughing.

"Oh, just shut up and drive. Brian's going to think we've forgotten to pick him up," I said.

Soon, we pulled into Brian's long, dark gravel driveway. We drove past his single-wide mobile home and straight to his workshop. His shop was where Brian kept his front-end loader, Bobcat skid-steer, and three large dump trucks. In the dim light from the only streetlight on his property, I saw a tall, skinny country boy standing by a gun case and a large rolling duffel bag.

"I thought you forgot me," Brian said as we slowly

pulled to a stop and opened the door to the truck.

"Did you remember your Texas hunting license and your locks for your gun case?" JP asked.

"I got everything I need except something to settle my nerves. I didn't sleep a wink last night," declared Brian. "I guess I'm just excited about the trip and the possibility of shooting a huge deer."

JP grabbed Brian's gun case and camo duffel bag and threw them into the back of the truck while Brian jumped into the backseat.

"Morning, Jack. Did you sleep any last night?" Brian asked.

"I slept like a baby. Let's go, JP. We still have to pick up Yeoman and be at the airport by six-thirty," I said.

On the way to Yeoman's house, Brian told us about his new Remington Mag 7 that his wife bought him for Christmas. "I've shot over a hundred rounds trying to zero this new gun in and make sure I can make a 250-yard shot," Brian explained.

"Two hundred fifty yards!" JP shouted. "I don't go that far on vacation, let alone try to kill a deer that far."

It took only about ten minutes to get to Yeoman's house, and it was apparent he had been waiting for some time. When we pulled into the driveway, we saw Yeoman fast asleep in his outdoor lounge chair with his gun case and bags next to him. When we pulled up to Yeoman, JP's headlights shone on his big frame, waking up the sleeping giant.

"Sorry to wake you, Yeoman. Have you been out here all night?" asked JP.

"I've been sleeping here since about three A.M., waiting on you guys. We should have left last night," said Yeoman. "If we had, this dreaded flight would be over and we would be hunting in Texas this morning."

I got out of the front seat of the truck, leaving the door open for Yeoman, knowing full well he was far too big to ride in the backseat.

"I can just ride in the back," said Yeoman.

"Yeah, right, Yeoman," I snickered.

"What's that supposed to mean?" said Yeoman.

"Never mind. Just get in the front and relax, Yeoman," I replied.

It took only about forty-five minutes to get to the airport, especially at that time on a Sunday morning. Not much was said on the way, and before we knew it our luggage and guns were checked and we all were waiting to get on the plane.

Delmar and Buford read Sunday morning's paper while Mike, Brian, and JP drank coffee with Larry Wyatt. Everyone was eating Krispy Kreme donuts, with the exception of me and Yeoman.

"Aren't you hungry?" I asked Yeoman.

"Nope. I'm scared to death to fly and can't imagine eating donuts at a time like this," Yeoman shuddered.

"Yeoman, just get on the plane, settle in, and go to sleep. Everything will be fine, and there's nothing to worry about," I said, trying to reassure my friend.

Our conversation was cut short when the flight attendant made the announcement that boarding was beginning.

Yeoman and I were the first to get on board, quickly followed by our fellow friends and hunters. Yeoman got into the seat close to the window, and I settled in the aisle seat next to him.

"First time flying in first class, Yeoman?" I asked.

"Yep, and only my second time flying at all," Yeoman said. He was completely white-faced and looked sick on his stomach.

Just then, the flight attendant came to our seats and asked, "Anything to drink before we take off, guys?"

"I'll have a coffee, black, and my big friend will have a double Jack and Coke," I said. "He needs something to settle his nerves down."

"Make that a triple Jack!" yelled Yeoman as the attendant turned to gather the drinks.

All the members of our hunting crew were in their first-class seats talking quietly in anticipation of the upcoming and long-awaited hunting trip. I thought that, with a triple Jack and lack of sleep, Yeoman would soon be in la-la land and unaware of the flight or much of anything.

"Yeoman, you don't drink whiskey," said Mike.

"I do right now," said Yeoman. "And until this plane lands, Jack Daniel's and I are going to comfort each other."

As the 737 roared violently, trying to get airborne,

I heard my friend Yeoman snoring, but not so loud as to disturb anyone else sitting close by.

"I see your friend has drifted off to sleep," the attendant said.

"Yes, ma'am. He hasn't slept much in the last few days in anticipation of this trip," I explained. "Would you like to help me make this a flight he and my friends will never forget?"

"What do you have in mind?" she asked.

"Please bring me the oxygen mask that you demoed when explaining the safety guidelines, then get in a safe place and watch this big man beside me," I snickered.

Soon, I stood over Yeoman wearing a demo oxygen mask while the flight attendant and my friends barely held their laughter. All the while, he slept ever so soundly. I braced myself, grabbed Yeoman's big arm, and shouted his name, muffled under the mask.

With sleepy eyes, Yeoman slowly woke, and all the passengers heard a loud, blood-curdling country yell. It was the longest "*Whoaaaaaaa!*" I had ever heard. The entire plane, including all our hunting buddies with the exception of Yeoman, burst into laughter.

When Yeoman regained his composure, which took at least twenty minutes, he swore, "It's way too early in the morning for that shit. And even if it takes me to the end of my time, I will get you back, Jack, and when you least expect it."

We had a direct flight into Corpus Christi, Texas, from Greensboro, which was about a three-and-a-half-hour trip. Soon, all the green below started turning a light brown, and I knew we were getting closer and closer to Texas every minute.

"Won't be long before we land," explained Mike. "I've been looking forward to this trip for a long time."

"Will Blaine meet us at the airport or the camp?" asked Delmar.

"Blaine will meet us at the camp," I answered. The camp was called "the South Texas Hilton." "We'll eat a spot of lunch and be in the deer stands by two P.M. their time."

The area we would hunt was just outside the small town of Hebbronville, Texas, about a two-hour drive from Corpus and about twenty-two miles from the town of Laredo and the Mexican border.

Just as I was about to order Yeoman a fresh Jack and Diet, the flight attendant announced that we had begun our descent and would be landing shortly. I looked out Yeoman's window and saw the ground fast approaching. Yeoman looked to be getting sick. As the plane's engines reversed and the pilot applied the brakes, Yeoman and my entire hunting crew had landed and were safe.

Yeoman proudly explained to all on the plane who would listen, "I never was scared. I just thought I would give you-all something to laugh about during the boring flight."

"Yeoman, you're so full of it your eyes are brown. Now, get off the plane and help me gather up the luggage," Mike said.

It took us a good hour to gather our luggage and guns, rent the cars, load up everything, and head for Hebbronville. Mike, Brian, Yeoman, and I rode together, while JP, Larry Wyatt, Delmar, and Buford partnered up in an SUV identical to ours. Our small convoy was on its way.

When we passed though the small town of Alice, Yeoman

spotted a chicken joint and announced to everyone, "I am starved to death. Let's stop for a quick bite, maybe a bucket or two."

"Good idea, Yeoman. But we're stopping beside this chicken place only to buy beer at the local Stop and Go," said Mike.

Both rental cars pulled into the Stop and Go, and I jumped out and ran inside, looking for the restroom. Mike and Brian were loading up on beer and snacks when I came out, just in time to help pay.

"Hey, where's Yeoman?" I asked.

"I think he got a dozen candy bars and headed back to the car," said Brian.

When we got to the car and loaded the beer into the backseat, Yeoman was not in sight.

"Hey, anybody seen Yeoman?" JP asked his dad and the others in his car.

"Yep. He went in the chicken joint next door. Where else would he be?" said Delmar.

Just then, Yeoman appeared, coming through the chicken joint's front door loaded down with three big buckets of his favorite, yard bird.

"Just needed a little something to tide me over until we get to the South Texas Hilton," said Yeoman.

We all just laughed and reached for the hot, crispy chicken from one of the buckets. The tops of cold beers opening could be heard for at least a city block.

Chapter Three

When we drove through the desert toward the deer camp, I couldn't help wondering what stories those old mesquite trees could tell, if only they could reveal all their past. I wondered how many Indians, Mexicans, and Americans perished trying to carve out a life in that godforsaken place. It appeared by the look of the desert that nothing—no animal, tree, grass, or man—could survive in that harsh environment. Maybe that's why folks loved that part of the country. When you first looked at it, you thought nothing, and I mean nothing, could live like that. Water had to be pumped out of deep holes in the ground and stored in huge, round concrete reservoirs. Those reservoirs supplied water not only to the longhorn cows on every ranch but also to every living creature in the desert. Everything—including the deer, foxes, quail, rabbits, coyotes, mountain lions, bobcats, wild boars, and every other animal—relied on the water holes for survival.

As I sat daydreaming about the desert, the South Texas Hilton deer camp came into sight. When we turned onto the dirt road leading to the camp, wild quail ran across the dirt road in front of our SUV.

Yeoman yelled, "Hey, stop and we'll shoot us some quail for dinner!"

"Yeoman, wake up and join the party. We have deer rifles, not shotguns," scolded Mike.

"Oh, yeah, all this fried chicken must have gone to my head," said Yeoman. "I wonder what we're having for dinner, anyway."

"Is eating all you think about?" asked Brian. "We're going to one of the finest deer-hunting camps in all of Texas, and all you can think about is eating."

"Hey, leave me alone. Do I have to put up with your bull

for three whole days?" Before Brian could answer, Yeoman asked, "Who is that near the fire pit?"

I first met Blaine twenty years earlier when I took three customers to Mexico bass fishing. I was so excited to have the opportunity to fish in Mexico that I couldn't sleep for days before we left the United States. I met my customers in the Atlanta airport, where we caught another flight to Brownsville, Texas. In the airport in Brownsville, I should have known something was wrong when nobody from the Mexican fishing lodge was there to pick us up. After a quick call to the owner's house, it wasn't long until a man about my age came running into the airport with a sign that had my name on it in big, bold letters. This was when I met Blaine, and neither he nor I was pleasant to one another.

"Why in the hell did you call the owner?" he asked. "I was running just a few minutes late. Shit, can't you damn Yankees wait a damn minute for nothing?"

"Hey, as much money as this trip cost, mister, I expect everything to be on time and perfect," I snapped back.

"Then you best just get your ass back on that plane and go back to where you and the rest of your Yankee friends came from," he blurted out.

I probably would have done just that, but I had already paid for the trip, and my customers were as excited as I was about the possibility of catching a world-record bass.

"Who the hell are you calling a Yankee? I'm just as Southern as you are," I said. Trying to smooth things over and calm the situation down, I added, "Let's just get our Southern asses in the car and have a beer and go fishing."

Blaine laughed, picked up a pile of fishing rods, tied them to the top of what had to be the oldest existing Suburban in the entire land of Dixie, and exclaimed, "I've had a few of those beers in my time. I guess one more won't hurt."

I agreed and thought to myself that he must have drunk those few beers that very day, and it was only eleven-thirty in the morning.

So there we went, rods on top, luggage in the back, customers in the backseat, me on the passenger side, Blaine driving, and a cooler of beer on the front seat between him and me. I don't know if it was the beer or Blaine's experience, but he drove through Mexico as if he had lived there all his life. It was constant pedal to the metal, cuss words flying out of Blaine's mouth. He stopped just long enough to let the beer go down.

We had gone only about twenty miles into Mexico when we were stopped at what appeared to be a Mexican army roadblock.

"Shit! Just my luck," Blaine yelled, the brake cylinders squealing as he tried to stop the moving pile of junk.

"What's going on? Why are they stopping us?" I asked Blaine.

"Boy, I can tell you've never been in Mexico. They want money," he angrily replied. "Why else would they stop a beat-up car with a bass painted on the side and a sign that says, 'World's Best Bass Fishing in Mexico,' and, most of all, a full load of Unites States Yankees?"

As the car rolled to a stop, a young man dressed immaculately in army fatigues motioned Blaine to roll down his window. Blaine, now about two sheets to the wind but trying to act sober, yelled, "Why are you stopping us? I have very important Americans in here, and we have urgent business in Victoria!"

Slowly, with an M16 rifle in hand, the young man said,

"Get out of the car, señor," while motioning all of us to do likewise. "Unload the car of everything. We are today searching for drugs, señor."

"Drugs!" Blaine yelled. "Why, you're a stupid idiot. Why would we bring drugs from the United States into Mexico?"

This question didn't a bit more get out of Blaine's drunken mouth than we were surrounded by at least twenty-five Mexican soldiers, all with new M16 rifles. Silence and fright were the only things in the air at that moment. I began contemplating how I was going to get myself and my customers out of this when the passenger door of a military vehicle parked close to us opened. Out stepped a beautiful young Mexican lady who I thought might be the captain of the unit.

Blaine, still in a half-drunken, mad stupor, said loudly, "Look at that bitch!"

Two hundred dollars later, we were back in the car on our way to fishing. I drove while Blaine was passed out in the passenger seat.

The rest of the trip went downhill fast. The fishing was terrible and the food and sleeping quarters worse, not to mention the ride back to Texas. In addition, Blaine got drunk every night and cried about all he had done in Vietnam—the men he had killed, the horrors he had seen, how he could see those people in his dreams. I thought any man would probably try to drink those memories away.

Years went by and I never heard from him until, one day, I received a phone call from Blaine. We talked for almost an hour. He explained how he had gotten married and had gone to counseling for years to stop the nightmares. He said he had even stopped drinking and moved to Texas and was making a living in the cow business.

Blaine and I had several conversations and formed a sort of friendship in time, over the phone. I followed Blaine and his family from the cow business to the hunting and fishing business. Blaine told me that the cow business in its heyday provided not just a living, but in fact had made him and his family quite wealthy. Over time, he had saved and invested his hard-earned cash in land and hunting leases. Investing in land was how he had gotten himself into the hunting and fishing business. He guided deer hunters on ranches he owned or leased, in addition to guiding fishermen in Baytown,

Texas. Blaine told me several times that the guiding business was a lot more fun and not nearly the work as cows, not to mention the better aroma.

There Blaine stood beside the fire pit, waiting on us to arrive. He had aged quite a bit since the last time I saw him in Mexico and had lost quite a bit of weight. But by his tall-drink-of-water stance, I could tell it was Blaine.

When the cars rolled to a gentle, dusty stop, I slowly opened the door and walked straight toward Blaine. "Hello again, my old friend," I said as I extended my right hand to shake his.

Blaine grabbed my hand with a big smile on his face and pulled me close, wrapping his huge arms around my back for a hug as big as Texas. "It's really good to see you again. You sure are fat!" Blaine barked all in one breath.

"Same old Blaine, so full of piss and vinegar your eyes are brown. You haven't changed in all these years," I said.

"That's where you're wrong, Jack. I don't drink as much as I used to, and I've forgotten all about the war and all the horrible things I've done," Blaine said.

I thought, *Here we go again. Blaine said he hasn't had a drink*

in years, and now I find out he hasn't stopped, only slowed down.
I just stood there looking at him sort of dumbfounded and decided this was not the time to discuss it. I wanted to have a great hunting trip for myself, my friends, and especially Yeoman, so I decided to bide my time and talk to Blaine later.

I hollered to my crowd of friends, "Hey, you guys come over here. I want you to meet my friend Blaine!"

All the guys except Yeoman slowly walked toward the fire pit where Blaine and I stood.

Blaine extended his hand and said, "I'm Blaine, and welcome to the South Texas Hilton."

First to meet Blaine was Mike Dillion, then JP, then Brian, his father, Larry, Delmar, and lastly Buford.

"Where's Yeoman?" I asked.

"After two hours of riding and one hour of stuffing his big belly with chicken, last I saw of Yeoman, he was looking for a bathroom," Mike laughed.

"Grab your things and find a bunk or a room. This is your home for the next three days," said Blaine.

Everyone scattered, grabbed their guns and bags, and headed into double-wide trailers hooked together by wooden walkways. As we approached the first set of trailers, we walked up a long flight of steps onto a wraparound front porch that had a hand-painted sign nailed to the wall. The sign was made of old, rustic mesquite wood and was just about head height. It dangled from a rusted chain and read, "Welcome to the South Texas Hilton." From the porch, we continued to walk through sliding glass doors into the kitchen and mess hall. The mess hall led into the common area, with sofas, chairs, and a wide-screen TV. In addition to all the comforts, there were lots of deer mounts on each wall, as well as quail, turkeys, wild hogs, and one huge rattlesnake. Close to the common area and leading to an adjoining deck and another trailer was a well-stocked bar with every kind of alcohol you could imagine. The normal path through this, the main trailer, was kitchen, mess hall, common area, and bar, leading eventually to a walkway to trailer #2. Trailers #2, #3, and #4 were all the same, with lots of double bunks, one common bathroom, and only one private bedroom and bath.

Once I walked into trailer #2 and saw the private bedroom, I called to everyone, "This is my bedroom, and all you guys keep out." That was when I noticed that someone had painted my name on a piece of cardboard and tacked it on the wall facing my private bedroom and bath.

I moved into the room, letting my eyes adjust from the bright Texas sky to a small, dark room. In the room were two bunk beds with green blankets on each. The air conditioner was blasting, which explained the blankets. There were also two wooden shelves attached to one wall for storage of clothes and hunting accessories. The adjoining room was a small but useful bathroom with a toilet, mirror, sink, and shower.

I immediately started to unpack and change into something cooler. When we left North Carolina that morning, the temperature was twenty-eight. In Hebbronville, the temperature was a hot, humid eighty-five. Bonnie told me she had packed a pair of shorts for just this occasion. In the very bottom of my hunting bag, I finally found a pair of khaki shorts and a green Bass Pro fishing T-shirt. When I pulled them free from all the other hunting clothes, a small piece of folded notebook paper fell out. On the outside of the paper in Bonnie's handwriting was, "To Jack." I chuckled when I read it. Who else did she think I would assume it was for? I sat on the lower bunk, opened the handwritten note, and read in a slight whisper, "Jack, I miss you already. Be safe, have fun, and remember I love you." We had been married for over thirty-three years, and she still thought of the little things that helped to bind our love and affection.

As I sat on my bunk thinking about Bonnie, I was startled by a quick rap on my door. Mike opened it and said, "Are you going to stay inside or come out and have a beer with us? Blaine wants each of us to shoot our rifles to make sure the scopes are still on. Guess he don't want a bunch of Davie County rednecks missing or, worse, wounding his deer."

"Okay, Mike, let me change into these shorts and I'll be right there," I said.

Mike added, "When you come out of trailer #2, don't turn left. Go straight through the bar and common area and back out the front door."

"Why can't I go left?" I asked.

"That's where we're going to be shooting the rifles, and you may get mistaken for a target," Mike explained.

While I was changing clothes, I heard the loud blast of the first shot from a Remington Mag 7. Soon, I was dressed and headed out of my trailer. I crossed a small deck and entered trailer #1 in the bar area. Once inside, my eyes had to refocus from the dim light of #2 into the bright Texas sun on the catwalk decking, then back to the dim light in the bar and common area of trailer #1. When my eyes adjusted to the dim light of the common area, I saw Blaine sitting on the sofa with a Miller Lite in his hand.

"Blaine, what the hell are you doing? It's only two o'clock and you're drinking. I thought you quit," I said.

"It's not my beer. Mike said you were coming out to zero in your rifle, so I got you a cold beer," explained Blaine.

I took the beer from Blaine, and it was cold and sealed. "Sorry, Blaine. It's just you said at the fire pit that you don't drink much anymore. When we talked in the past, you told me you had quit for good," I said.

"Jack, I did quit for good a few years back, but through counseling I've realized that I can drink occasionally without ill effects," Blaine replied. "In fact, I have not had a bad dream about Vietnam in years. So I enjoy a cold beer or sometimes a Jack and Diet, but only after dark and work. I never get drunk anymore."

I just shrugged my shoulders and continued through the common area into the mess hall and ultimately out the same door where we first entered when we arrived.

As I walked out onto the decking of trailer #1, the loud crack of another rifle shot seemed to wake the whole desert.

Yeoman came around the corner of the trailer and asked me to come help him shoot his rifle. "My scope is not on," he said. "I shot at least a foot to the right, as well as about two inches high."

"I guess the scope got bumped from the luggage handlers on the plane," I said.

Slowly, Yeoman and I walked to the back side of all the trailers, and I saw Mike, JP, and Brian standing behind a shooting table. Each had a cold Miller Lite in one hand and a rifle in the other. About a hundred yards down range from the shooting table was a high mound of Texas dirt with targets in front. On the shooting table were two resting arms, one for the front of the rifle and the other to hold down the stock of the gun when fired.

I took Yeoman's Remington 247 and placed it on the supports on the shooting table. "Yeoman, you sure you want me to check your gun and adjust the scope?" I said.

"Well, sure I do. You can see better than me, and quite frankly you're the only one in this group I trust," said Yeoman.

"What do you mean, the only one you trust?" I asked.

"Well, all these other a-holes would love to see me miss a trophy buck, so I'm sure they'd fix my scope to shoot way off," said Yeoman.

"BS," Brian laughed. "We don't have to fix your gun. You couldn't hit a bull in the ass with a silver spade if you tried."

Everyone around the shooting table laughed at Brian's joke.

"Seriously, Yeoman, what's right for me may not be right for you. My arms are longer than yours, and much smaller in size," I said.

"Here we go again with the fat jokes. Do you want to help me or not?" said Yeoman.

Without a reply, I took Yeoman's 247 in hand and asked for a bullet. I opened the breech of the gun and slid a new round of Remington ammo into the barrel. "Fire in the hole!" I yelled as I sat down at the shooting table. Carefully, I slipped the safety off while aligning the crosshairs in Yeoman's scope with the target down range. Slowly, I pulled the trigger, and the gun exploded as the powder of the bullet ignited.

Mike stood behind me, looking through a pair of Burris binoculars at the target down range. He said, "That's a perfect shot, Jack, dead balls on center and two inches high at a hundred yards."

Yeoman complained, "How can it be perfect, dead balls on, when you just said it was two inches high?"

Blaine rounded the corner of the trailer and explained, "Two inches high at a hundred means that, at three hundred yards, the bullet will drop and hit dead balls on target."

"I can't hit a deer at three hundred yards. Hell, I don't even go on vacation that far, much less try to shoot a deer," Yeoman laughed. "Three hundred yards, that's bullshit."

Blaine announced, "Mr. Roy has a snack prepared for you in the front yard by the fire pit. You probably should eat a little something to last you till supper. We'll hunt till dark, then return to camp and cook steaks on the fire pit."

Everyone gathered their guns, beer, and other belongings. When we walked around the corner of trailer #1, I stopped to take a close look at the front yard of the South Texas Hilton. The entire yard was covered with remnants of earth-tone carpet. The carpet remnants were laid on the desert floor to keep the dust and mud out of the camp. It rained only about fifteen inches per year at the South Texas Hilton, but when it did the desert floor turned to mud. When it didn't rain, the wind could easily kick up dust clouds and ruin any food cooking on the fire pit. The carpet acted as a shield against dust, mud, and desert critters. There was only one tree in camp. It was a mesquite tree in the middle of the carpeted yard. It looked crooked, worn, and old. Alongside the tree was a long, neatly stacked row of split mesquite logs ready for the fire pit and cooking. In front of the tree was what Blaine called the fire pit. This was where most all suppers were cooked and where every tale and hunting lie was told. The fire pit was simply a three-by-five-foot hole dug into the desert with fire bricks lining the bottom, sides, and border above ground. Blaine had constructed a stainless-steel grate with legs that sat down into the fire pit for cooking. After the meal, the cooking grate was removed and more wood added, making a great campfire. Surrounding the pit were about a dozen white plastic chairs with the Walmart price tags still visible. Next to the pit was a folding white table where Mr. Roy had assembled an array of brisket biscuits, chips, salsa, guacamole, refried beans, tortillas, paper plates, and eating utensils.

Blaine announced, "After eating, everyone should meet here to be driven to your deer stands. Make sure you visit our snack bar in the common area for candy bars, crackers, and other snacks to carry with you to your stand. Also, each person should take at least two bottles of water, just in case we're late picking you up after the hunt."

"What do you mean, late?" asked Yeoman. "You mean it may be dark, and I might be all alone in my deer stand in the middle of the desert, in the middle of Texas, close to Mexico?"

Blaine tried to reassure Yeoman. "We may be looking for someone's shot deer, but we won't forget you, Yeoman. You'll be just fine."

Yeoman was then satisfied. He grabbed two plates and began loading them up with biscuits and a taste of everything Mr. Roy had prepared.

When I left the group and headed toward my room, Mike yelled, "Hey, Jack, where are you going?"

"Going to find a can of Beanee Weenee and some crackers," I explained.

"Bring me one," Mike begged. "I didn't bring any Tums, so I can't eat what's on Mr. Roy's table. Can you spare a can of beans for an old friend?"

"Sure, I'll grab extra if you'll make us a plate of crackers and chips," I said.

Thirty minutes later, everyone was dressed in camo hunting clothes, boots, blaze orange vest, and hat, waiting to be taken to their respective deer stands. The guides loaded the F-250 pickups with our guns, coolers of water, and deer corn to be put out within a hundred yards of each stand. In Texas, the best way to hunt deer was by spreading deer feed down each *sandero* close to the deer stand. A *sandero* was nothing more than a small road or winding path cut through the desert. It was used for transportation as well as being a feeding ground for deer and other animals. Deer stands were placed where two or more *sanderos* crossed, which enabled hunters to have access to several lanes of deer. The guides' trucks were loaded with deer corn to be spread on the desert trails, enabling the deer to eat and the hunters to shoot the deer of a lifetime.

"Doesn't seem like much of a challenge, shooting deer as they come out into the road to eat," said Yeoman.

"Not much at all, but can you make the shot?" Blaine asked. "Can you control your nerves? Can you control your breathing? Can you move and not be seen? Can you really make the shot, Yeoman?"

"I know it can be nerve-racking, but it still seems like not much of a challenge at all," said Yeoman.

"Yeah, you're right," said Blaine. "It's nothing like I lived through in Vietnam. 'Course, I was hunting something different than deer, and my quarry could shoot back."

Everyone was shocked at what Blaine said. We all just stood there with nothing but silence between us.

Trying to change the subject, I asked Yeoman, "Did you get a candy bar and water?"

Without answering, Yeoman opened his hunting coat to reveal dozens of candy bars, packs of crackers, and cold brisket biscuits, along with four bottles of water.

"Looks like you just robbed a convenience store, Yeoman," I said.

Everyone laughed as we loaded into the guides' trucks to go hunting.

Chapter Four

Mike, Yeoman, and I were in Blaine's truck. Of course, because of his size, Yeoman was riding shotgun, with Mike and me in the backseat. Delmar, Buford, and Larry Wyatt were in a white Ford F-250 with a guide everyone called Rip. Rip was dressed in cowboy boots, jeans, flannel shirt, and cowboy hat, and all this was covered by a green poncho. Rip looked like he had just walked out of the desert a hundred years ago. All the other guides at the camp said Rip was the best and knew exactly where all the big bucks were. The final truck to leave camp was one with a guide named Skipper. Skipper, was Blaine's younger brother. Skipper was better known for arrowhead hunting than deer hunting. In Skipper's truck was the rest of our Davie County crew—JP and our country redneck, Brian.

Blaine did not waste any time, speeding down a large *sandero*, dust flying and lots of roadrunners hurrying to get out of the way. Then Blaine turned right onto a much smaller *sandero* and headed deeper into the desert. As we rode, I saw deer stands scattered throughout the flat, dry, parched desert. Blaine commented that each stand had a deer feeder located within a hundred yards of shooting distance. A deer feeder in Texas consisted of a fifty-gallon drum sitting on an iron tripod that had a timer attached to release feed at a set time. Most were set to release deer feed right at daybreak and again when the sun began to set. The deer eventually became used to listening for the sound of the feed being dispensed from the feeders. Some of the guides said deer could even tell the exact time that feed would be thrown out. Once they heard those sounds, deer would come from the desert in all directions to feed. Rabbits, quail, and other desert animals also came to feast on the corn. The biggest shooter bucks were smart and tried to remain in the desert, where they were protected from hunters and predators. Just before daylight and just after dark, the biggest bucks came out from the cover of the desert to feed. This, of course, was generally the rule, but all bets were off when the big bucks came into rut and the does were in estrus.

It became evident to me very quickly there was no way Ycoman was going to be able to get into one of those stands. Each stand appeared to be a four-by-five-foot wooden box covered with a tin roof. There were shaded windows on each side. The windows slid down to open, which enabled the hunter to shoot a deer in any direction. All the deer stands looked to be about twenty to thirty feet off the ground, with steps that led to a small wooden door in the front of the stand.

"Yeoman, we have a problem," I said. "You can't climb three steps without a handrail on each side."

Blaine interrupted, "Yeoman will be the first to get out of the truck, and he will hunt the stand we call 'Fifth and Broad.'"

"Why do you call it Fifth and Broad?" I asked.

Blaine responded, "Well, we have a wide *sandero*, hence

the name *Broad*, which intersects five smaller *sanderos*, with Yeoman's ground blind right in the middle of the intersection."

Yeoman was the first to respond. "Ground blind, that's great. I was already dreading the climb into those other stands, not to mention trying to get down out of them at dark."

A picture of Yeoman falling down the steps and rolling across the desert floor ran through my mind, making me smile.

Soon, the dense desert opened up to a large, clean area about the size of three or four football fields. Just as Blaine said, there were five small *sanderos* intersecting with one large, wide road. On the ground was what appeared to be a large, round camo dome. It looked exactly like an igloo or dog box, with one door and windows that encircled the entire blind. Yeoman opened the door of the pickup as Mike and I jumped out of the backseat to help him get situated in his hunting blind. Yeoman opened the door to the igloo, looked inside, and saw benches encircling the entire enclosure. In the middle was a folding lawn chair that Yeoman could use to relax while looking all the way to the end of each *sandero* in a 360-degree circle.

"I should be able to shoot a Texas record buck from this stand," whispered Yeoman.

"Yeah, if you don't go to sleep after eating and sitting in that comfortable lawn chair," said Mike.

As Mike and I turned to get back into the truck, I said, "Yeoman, be careful. You know lawn chairs and you don't mix."

Yeoman smiled and mouthed the words, "Kiss my . . . ," but stopped short of completing what was the obvious.

Next, we dropped off Mike at a high tree stand overlooking three intersecting *sanderos*. Mike saw the Texas desert that seemed to go to the ends of the earth.

When Mike got out of the truck and prepared to climb the steps to his blind, Blaine whispered, "Mike, you can see Mexico from there. You can never be too careful. Sometimes, illegals cross the border and come right by this stand, headed to town to catch a ride north. Nothing to worry about. If you see anyone, just don't let them get onto the ladder of your stand."

Mike asked, "Why would they want to get into my stand?"

Blaine replied, "First, we always keep water in each stand. Second, for shelter. And finally, to hide from the Border Patrol. But they are harmless, just poor people looking for a better way of life. If you see a group, just wave them on."

Soon, we left Mike, and only Blaine and I were in the truck.

Blaine spoke first. "I'm putting you in the blind we call 'the Crow's Nest.' It's a very high blind in the intersection of four *sanderos*. We feed more deer corn at this stand than at any of the other locations on the ranch."

Just as Blaine said, as we approached the stand, deer were already out feeding in the *sanderos*. Most all were does, with a few spike bucks and some four-pointers as well. Spikes, called "cow horns" back home, typically belonged to very young deer with two straight horns on their heads.

When the truck slowed to a stop and I opened the door to get out, all the deer vanished into the desert brush. Quickly, I got my gun and water and climbed to my four-by-five box for the afternoon and evening. When I opened the door and attempted to enter, my eyes had to adjust to the darkness inside. Then I opened one of the windows to let light and fresh air into my hunting spot. I closed the door and latched the lock from the inside, remembering what Blaine had told Mike regarding the illegals.

As Blaine drove away, he said, "See you at dark. If you shoot a deer, send me a text and we'll come help retrieve it. Do not wander away from this deer stand. Everything in this desert will stick you, sting you, or bite you. Be careful, and shoot straight."

Resting in my lounge chair, I opened the remaining three windows while I put on my sunglasses. I was ready. All I had to do was relax, rest my mind, and wait for a monster buck to meet his fate.

CHAPTER FIVE

The dust that Blaine's truck kicked up had not even settled when I saw my first deer. It was only about fifty yards from my stand when it crept out of the brush. I saw it was a small doe. I was really surprised that I didn't see white spots on her fur. She was so young I bet she was still nursing.

It wasn't long before all four *sanderos* were filled with does and real small bucks. I had not seen this many deer in my entire hunting life, much less all at one time. Only problem, there was not a shooter or trophy buck in sight. I looked at my watch, and it was four o'clock. I had been in the stand only about an hour, and it was a long time till dark. My next thought was, *It won't be long until I'll have to text Blaine, Mike, Delmar, JP, Brian, Larry, Buford, and finally Yeoman that a big buck is down.*

Or so I thought! For the next few hours, I watched does, young bucks, quail, doves, roadrunners, and wild hogs feasting on corn and playing in the brush. It was absolutely beautiful, and it will always be a fond memory, but I did not see one shooter buck. Soon, the sun was setting in the west and I saw the lights of Blaine's truck approaching. Deer began to run, as if to say, *Here comes the man. Time to get out of sight.*

Blaine pulled up and parked on the *sandero* close to my deer stand's ladder. I gathered up my things and opened the door for the steep descent down the stairs.

Blaine held a bright flashlight to help guide my way.

Mike said, "I'll help put your stuff in the back of the truck."

When Blaine opened the pickup door, I saw Yeoman sitting in the front passenger seat watching me and Mike struggling with all the gear. Soon, everything was loaded.

I climbed into the backseat of the truck and said, "I got

this, Yeoman, but thanks for the help, anyway."

"Don't mention it," said Yeoman. "See any shooters?"

I replied, "Nope. Lots of does and a few small bucks, but no shooters."

Mike added, "Same here."

While we rode back to camp through the dark desert, the headlights of Blaine's truck showed all kind of animals living in that godforsaken place. We saw, of course, deer and hogs, but I was surprised when we saw javelinas, foxes, coyotes, and an occasional bobcat.

Blaine said, "There are lots of different critters living off the desert, or living off what is living in the desert."

Far away through the brush, I saw the lights and the campfire at the South Texas Hilton. Soon, we pulled in front of trailer #1, onto the carpet, and into Blaine's parking space. Attached to the main trailer was a stand-alone open shed used for skinning animals and cleaning game such as deer, quail, doves, and hogs. The shed was approximately twenty by twenty feet, with a metal roof and a concrete floor with a drain for blood. Under the shed and attached to the rafters were several hoists used for attaching deer or hogs for skinning and cleaning processes. All the chairs arranged in the cleaning shed were empty, and most all of our hunting buddies sat around a roaring fire in the pit. A quick glance at the hoist inside the cleaning shed told me that no one was successful in that afternoon's hunt.

Around the fire pit sat JP, Brian, Larry, Buford, and Delmar. When I got out of the truck, I yelled to my friends, "Did y'all not see anything, or did you just not shoot straight?"

Brian answered for the crowd: "We all saw lots of deer, just no shooters."

"Most bucks we saw had small baskets or cow horns. No shooters!" yelled Delmar.

I moved to the back of Blaine's truck and gathered my gear. With my arms full, I headed to my room, passing through trailer #1, where Mr. Roy was preparing the side dishes for supper.

"What you cooking, Mr. Roy?" I asked.

"Baked potatoes, onions with cheese, salad, and few special Mexican dips," said Mr. Roy.

Once I got to my room, I unloaded all my gear and put my gun on the gun rack under the shelf on the wall. I took off my hunting boots and clothes and changed into shorts, T-shirt, and tennis shoes. Then I sat on my bed and called Bonnie.

Just after the first ring, Bonnie answered and said what she always said: "Hey, honey." She asked me about my day and if the guys had a good time hunting and relaxing. I told her what a great day I had, and also that I loved and missed her something terrible. Next, she asked what we were having for supper. I told her that I didn't know for sure, but I thought it was steak because Mr. Roy said he had cooked baked potatoes and fixed a salad.

After about a fifteen-minute conversation, I said, "Guess I need to get outside with the rest of the crowd and see what's going on and hear all their stories or lies. Love you, miss you, and I'll call again after lunch tomorrow. Have a good night's sleep, and dream of me." That ended our first phone call of many over the next couple of days.

I strolled back through the common area and through the mess hall area and back onto the front porch. I looked toward the fire pit, and the entire gang was drinking beer and sitting around a huge campfire. When I joined the group, Mike handed me a Miller Lite and pulled up an empty chair for me to sit.

Yeoman spoke first to me, and I was surprised that what he said had nothing to do with the day's adventure. Instead, Yeoman said, "What time is supper going to be ready? I just about starved to death in that igloo today."

"Yeoman, how can you possibly be hungry? Your coat looked like you robbed a 7-Eleven store, and I know you had at least six brisket biscuits before you left camp," I said.

Yeoman explained, "Well, that was at least four hours ago and, not seeing any big deer, I got bored and ate everything up in the first thirty minutes in the stand."

I, along with all the rest of the crowd, just laughed.

Mike said, "Blaine, don't you have some snacks ready for Yeoman? The big dog needs to eat."

Blaine, without saying a word, brought over to the group a big tray of nachos covered with beef, cheese, refried beans, and, best of all, lots of jalapeños.

Mike said, "There you go, big boy, but be careful with all those jalapeños and beans. You might set your bunk on fire in your sleep."

Everybody laughed with a big roar except Yeoman.

"Okay, guys, let's change the subject and promise not to talk about eating or fat jokes. I came to have a nice hunting vacation," said Yeoman.

Trying to make my friend feel better, I said, "What was the biggest buck you guys saw today?"

Larry Wyatt was the first to answer. "I saw a ton of shooter bucks if we were still in Davie County, but nothing that would not be laughed at if you shot it in Texas."

Mike, JP, Brian, Buford, and Delmar pretty much had the same answer.

Yeoman added, "Even though I didn't see any big bucks, I had a great time watching all the other game in the desert. But my favorite was the wild hogs."

"Why?" I asked.

Yeoman quickly answered, "Those pigs lined up across the *sandero* and ate every kernel of corn in the road all the way to my hunting igloo. They sucked up that corn like they had a vacuum cleaner attached to their snout."

"You mean sort of like you, Yeoman, at Jack's shed when he serves a big platter of peel-and-eat shrimp?" said Delmar.

"Hey, I thought we said no fat jokes or talk about my

eating," said Yeoman.

"Sorry, Yeoman. I couldn't help myself. I'll try to do better," said Delmar.

After lots of beer, steaks, salads, and baked potatoes, everyone's hunger was gone as the night grew late. Blaine, with a Jack and Diet in his hand, said, "Okay, guys, five A.M. comes early. Y'all better hit the sack. Mr. Roy will wake you up at least by five for breakfast, and we'll leave the camp before daylight for another exciting day hunting at the South Texas Hilton."

Everyone got up from the fire pit and headed toward their respective bunks. When I got into the kitchen area of trailer #1, I looked back outside toward the fire pit. I saw Blaine pick up a bottle of Jack Daniel's and headed toward his room. I thought, *Blaine might not be able to answer the bell at five in the morning. I just hoped he wouldn't show his ass and ruin my and my friends' Texas hunt.*

The next sound I heard was someone pounding on my bedroom door. "Who is it?" I yelled.

"It's Mr. Roy, and breakfast will be ready in thirty minutes," he replied.

I jumped out of my bunk and headed to the bathroom. I was excited to get ready for what I hoped would be a great day in the desert hunting deer and watching all the birds and critters trying to survive in that unforgiving terrain.

Chapter Six

I was the first of our group to arrive in the mess hall area, and much to my surprise there sat Blaine at the main table. "Hope you slept well," Blaine said as I brewed my first cup of coffee.

"I sure did, Blaine. Hope you did as well," I said, hoping to get the day started off right. I was such a big coffee fan that I had Bonnie ship my Keurig coffee maker all the way to Texas for this hunting trip. Good thing, too, because my beer-drinking buddies had to drink several cups to clear their heads after last night's gathering at the fire pit.

Next to arrive looking for coffee were Delmar and Buford,

then JP and Mike, followed by Brian, Larry, and finally, pulling up the rear, Yeoman. Yeoman came into the room with a sneaky grin on his face and announced that he had a crazy dream last night.

"Tell us all about it, Yeoman," Mike said as he poured his first cup of coffee.

"Well, you know I told you guys back at Jack's shed that I am on this Atkins Diet, and I had eaten so much chicken. Well, last night, I had a nightmare that I was chasing and eating live chickens as fast as I could catch them," said Yeoman, somewhat excited.

"Man, that's gross," said Buford.

Then Yeoman raised his cupped hand to his mouth and said, "Wonder what in the world would make someone dream such a horrible dream." At the same time, he coughed, and out of his hand flew torn pieces of white Kleenex that looked just like chicken feathers. Everyone in the mess hall area burst into a tremendous roar of laughter while choking on hot coffee.

When things finally calmed down, Mike asked, "Yeoman, where in the world do you come up with this stuff? Did you sit up all night plotting this crazy story?"

"Yep," was Yeoman's only answer.

Mr. Roy yelled from the kitchen, "Breakfast is ready! Grab you a plate and come fill it up. Eat as much as you want."

We formed a line from the mess hall area into the kitchen. When I walked around the corner, I saw a long table that Mr. Roy had prepared with all kinds of breakfast foods. At the end was a griddle where he was prepared to cook your eggs to order. First on the table were napkins and eating utensils, followed by a big bowl of assorted cut fruit. Next was a big aluminum pan filled with crisp bacon, country ham, and fried sausage. Next was another big aluminum pan filled with partially cooked canned biscuits that looked like they had passed close to the stove but not cooked for very long.

"Didn't imagine we'd be having dough balls with our bacon and eggs this morning," whispered Larry Wyatt.

Quickly, I whispered back, "If Mr. Roy hears you, he may send you home with something that Pepto-Bismol or Imodium can't fix."

Larry burst out laughing, and Mr. Roy wanted to know what was so funny. Larry said, "Nothing, Mr. Roy. I'm still laughing at Yeoman's chicken joke." Mr. Roy looked like he didn't believe Larry but let it go for the time being.

After eating a big breakfast and watching Yeoman return to the chow line three times, I got up and looked outside to see if I could determine what the weather might be for the day. It was pitch dark, so I asked Blaine, "What can we expect weather-wise during this morning's hunt?"

Blaine said, "The weather today will be hot, with highs close to eighty-five degrees and wind blowing from the south at fifteen to twenty miles per hour."

"Not the best deer-hunting weather, guys, but that's why they call it hunting and not killing," I said. I thought that at least it would be comfortable in the deer stand if I wore short sleeves and if the wind blew enough to keep me somewhat cool. In addition, at least I knew I would see lots of deer, and hopefully the quail and all the other critters would return to munch on the corn scattered for the deer.

"Daylight will be in forty-five minutes, so everyone be in your respective guides' trucks in fifteen minutes to deliver your butts to the deer stands," Blaine announced.

Mr. Roy added, "Don't forget to take snacks and at least

two bottles of water because you won't be back here for lunch until just before twelve o'clock."

Blaine continued to give instructions. "If you should shoot a deer, do not get out of your stand. Just watch the way he runs so we can pick up the blood trail later and track your trophy."

JP asked, "Why do we have to stay in our stand after we kill a deer? I want to get out of that hot box and look for my deer."

"Well, if you want to, JP, be my guest," said Blaine. "But when you get bit by a six-foot rattlesnake, don't come crying to me. In fact, if that happens, when we find you, chances are you'll have already died."

One of the other guides, called Old Man Jack, added, "Everything in this desert will either stick you, sting you, or bite you, and lots of those critters and things are deadly."

JP then said, "Well, since you put it that way, I guess I could stay a little longer in my stand. Maybe it won't be that uncomfortable."

Soon, everyone was loaded into their respective guides' trucks and headed down dark *sanderos* with hopes of killing the biggest deer of their life.

Shortly after daybreak, the same large group of wild hogs I saw yesterday came down the same *sandero*, vacuuming up every last kernel of corn. I kept thinking that if I didn't see a shooter buck by the end of tomorrow's hunt, one of those big, old pigs would be riding in the back of Blaine's truck. I thought it would be nothing for me to shoot a pig and have Mr. Roy butcher it for the next group to feast on when they came to the South Texas Hilton.

Blaine's weather report was correct, at least in my deer stand. It was hotter than Hades. The wind picked up, as he reported, but it did little to cool the temps in my blind. That morning's hunt was similar to the previous afternoon's hunt. I saw a lot of small bucks and twice as many young does, all the while swatting wasps that flew in one window of my deer blind and out another. That day's hunt was not very pleasant because of the heat, the wasps, and especially the lack of shooter bucks. It seemed like forever, but finally 11:15 rolled around and I saw Blaine's truck kicking up the dirt and dust from the dry desert floor. Soon, the truck rolled to a stop close to the same place as yesterday evening. When I started down from my stand, I met Blaine coming up the ladder to help carry my gear. When I finally reached the bottom of the stand, I looked in the truck and saw that Blaine had already picked up Mike and Yeoman. Yeoman's big frame was on the front seat, and Mike was resting in the back.

Before I even got settled into the truck, Yeoman asked, "See anything worth shooting at?"

"Not unless you count a bunch of small bucks, does, quail, and a big herd of hogs," I replied.

Mike joined in. "Jack, it's not a herd of hogs. The proper name for a group of wild hogs is a sounder of swine."

"Well, I didn't know you were so educated, Mike. I'm very impressed," I added.

"Not really. I had the same luck as you, and being that I was bored to death, I Googled it on my phone while sitting in my sauna hunting house," Mike confessed.

We all snickered at Mike's response.

Yeoman added, "Dang, Mike, I was truly impressed with your knowledge of pigs. You should have kept your mouth shut."

As we got closer to camp, I saw that our truck was the

last to arrive. All the other guys sat close to the old, crooked mesquite tree, fighting for a bit of shade. JP was dressed in a sloppy T-shirt, cut-off sweat pants, and flip-flops. He was drinking a Miller Lite.

As Yeoman got out of the truck, he announced, "Dang, JP, you look comfortable. I think I'll go put on my fat boy short pants, too. Someone fetch me a beer, would you?"

Blaine quickly replied, "Yeoman, I'll get you a real cold one out of the cooler. We have cases of Miller Lite on ice for just this kind of occasion." Blaine headed toward a huge white cooler sitting on the porch at the top of the stairs and reached way down into the ice, retrieving two ice-cold Miller Lites.

As I was getting all my stuff out of the truck, I yelled, "No thanks, Blaine. I think I'll just have a bottle of water."

Blaine laughed and said, "Wasn't getting you a cold beer. This one is for me. I'm about to burn up."

Before I could react, Mr. Roy came onto the porch from the kitchen area and announced that lunch was served.

Mike turned to the crowd and said, "It's so damn hot, I think I'll just have a snack and sit out under this tree and drink beer until it's time to go back hunting. No lunch for me."

Blaine said, "That's a great idea, Mike. I think I'll join you. Mr. Roy, please bring Mike and me some chips and a bowlful of your famous salsa, as well as a six-pack of Miller."

I just thought, *Whatever*, and headed into trailer #1, going through the common area and out onto the small porch that led into trailer #2. When I entered the dark sleeping trailer, I paused to let my eyes adjust, all the while enjoying the rush of cool air coming from all the air-conditioning vents. Once inside my bedroom, I sat on my bed and called Miss Bonnie.

After about five rings, she finally answered the phone. Using her sweetest voice, she said, "Hello, honey."

I responded, "Hey, baby. What are you doing?"

"Oh, it's you. I thought it was my boyfriend calling to let me know he was on his way here," she said, all the while snickering.

All I said was, "Funny!"

"It's a joke, stupid. Who tinkled in your corn flakes this morning?" she growled.

"Sorry, baby. It's hotter than hell down here, and we're

not seeing any deer big enough to shoot," I reported. "In fact, most all the deer I saw looked like they were still nursing tit. And to top all that off, Blaine was drinking beer out in the front yard with Mike."

"You just said it's hotter than hell there, so don't be so hard on Blaine. He'll probably only have one and will be ready to take you back deer hunting after lunch," Bonnie said, trying to reassure me to calm down and enjoy my time in Texas.

"Yeah, honey, I'm sure you're right. I'm going to put on some shorts and go to the mess hall for lunch and shoot the bull with the guys before this afternoon's hunt," I said.

Bonnie asked, "What time are you going back out hunting?"

"Probably, since it's so hot, we might wait until close to four this afternoon," I replied.

Bonnie said, "Okay, call me when you get in tonight so I won't worry. I hope you get a shot at a big buck this evening."

After I changed into my shorts and T-shirt that Bonnie packed, I headed back into the common area and finally into the mess hall, where all the guys were already eating and telling about their morning's hunt.

Yeoman said, "I bet I saw a hundred small deer. All were either does or small bucks. Back in Davie County, most of them would have been shooters, but here in Texas I'm going to wait on a monster buck."

"Hey, where's Blaine?" I asked.

Mike said, "Last time I saw him, he was sitting out front in the shade drinking a cold beer."

I stood up and looked through one of the windows in the mess hall toward the old mesquite tree. I saw Blaine asleep in one of those white plastic Walmart chairs, surrounded by what looked like a dozen or so empty beer cans lying on the desert ground. I was now pissed. I thought, *Blaine won't be driving me, Mike, and Yeoman anywhere this afternoon.* Even if he woke up, there was no way I was going to get into that truck with Blaine. God only knew where I might end up.

When I got my plate and headed toward the chow line, I saw Mr. Roy serving pork ribs with baked beans, coleslaw, fried potatoes, and hushpuppies. When I got closer, I asked if he had a truck I could borrow for the afternoon hunt.

Mr. Roy quickly answered, "Why do you need a truck? You're riding with Blaine this afternoon, aren't you?"

I just motioned for Mr. Roy to step over to the window and look for himself at the kind of condition Blaine was in, and it was only twelve-thirty.

Mr. Roy looked out the window and shook his head in disappointment. "Blaine is my closest friend, not to mention he is also my employer. I love the man as much if he were my very own son," he added. "You know Blaine has some real issues, and drinking all the time doesn't help the situation."

"What situation?" I asked Mr. Roy.

"I think Blaine is still living in 1967 in Vietnam, with all the carnage he lived through during the war," he answered.

"Blaine told me he went to counseling for several years, and all that was behind him, including the drinking," I said.

"Well, unfortunately, Blaine was lying," said Mr. Roy. "When Blaine first returned home, he did go to counseling and started taking the medicines the veterans hospital doctors prescribed. He seemed to be getting better and getting his life back together. He even started the hunting and fishing guide business and did really well until the last two or three years. Now, it seems he's about to lose his home and all his hunting leases simply because he can't leave the bottle alone. Blaine has been drunk for at least two years, and I was hoping that you guys coming to hunt would change him, at least for a couple of days."

"I am so sorry, Mr. Roy. I, too, was hoping for a few days of fun and sun with this crazy group from North Carolina," I said. "If I had known, I wouldn't have planned this trip. If you can get me a truck to use for this afternoon's hunt, I'll take the guys out to their deer stands, and I'll park the truck close to my stand for the return to camp."

"No problem. What time do you think you'll be heading out to hunt?" said Mr. Roy.

"We'll leave camp at four, and I'm hoping it will cool down some by then. It's hotter than hell," I said.

I went back into the mess hall, where Yeoman and the rest of our group were enjoying their after-meal dessert, consisting of homemade pecan pie with a big scoop of cold vanilla ice cream on top.

I said, "Dang, that looks good."

Yeoman said, "You're darn straight it's good. This is my

third piece."

"Well, Yeoman, stop eating for just a moment. I have something important to discuss with you and the group. Guys, listen up." All eyes from my friends and neighbors were looking at me and waiting to hear what was so darn important to interrupt their dessert. "Look out the window at Blaine," I said.

Several of my friends close to the windows stood and looked at Blaine passed out under the mesquite tree in the front yard.

Mike spoke first. "Looks like Blaine had a snootful, and it's just lunchtime."

"Yeah, you're right, Mike. Looks like Blaine won't be able to answer this afternoon's bell," I added. I then confessed that Blaine and I had a history that dated back many years. I went on to tell them the whole story about the time we met in Mexico on a bass-fishing excursion to Lake Aqua Milpa. I told them Blaine stayed drunk the whole trip and ruined it for my customers. I continued to tell them how Blaine had cried about all the people he killed in Vietnam and about all the nightmares he suffered. He had killed not just soldiers, but also women and children, and Blaine had confessed that he drank every day to forget. Blaine also told me he thought there was no way God would forgive all he had done.

"That's terrible. Maybe I should go talk to him," replied Yeoman.

I said, "Yeoman, here's what I think we should do. It's hotter that hell down here, the hunting was fun but terrible, and no one has seen anything to shoot except maybe a hog or two. I think we should finish this afternoon's hunt and come back to camp and have a nice steak dinner. Then we'll get a good night's sleep and head home tomorrow morning. Besides, nothing we can say or do will change Blaine, nor should we try."

Mike said, "I agree the hunting sucks, and we're out here in the middle of nowhere just waiting on something worse to happen. Let's just cut this trip short and go home and hopefully plan a Virginia turkey hunt for spring."

Larry Wyatt agreed and said, "After this afternoon's hunt and dinner, we'll pack up our gear and leave for the airport at first light, right?"

"Yep, that's the plan, if all agree," I said. I heard a few

mumbles, but all agreed to finish this terrible trip early and go home.

I returned to my room to rest on my bunk and try to get cool. As I lay there, I couldn't help feeling sorry for Blaine and all he had gone through. I truly thought he had recovered from all those nightmares, as well as given up drinking. Boy, was I fooled. I should have come down to Texas myself and checked things out before I had all my friends waste their time and money on a hunting trip from hell.

I was shocked out of deep thought when Mike banged on my door and asked, "Are you asleep? It's four, and we're waiting on you in the truck."

"Sorry, I'll be right there," I said to Mike.

Slowly, I got out of my bunk, gathered up my hunting stuff, and headed back into the common area of trailer #1. There, lying on the sofa and snoring loudly from the booze, was Blaine, completely oblivious to what was going on around him.

Mr. Roy was in the dining area cleaning up from lunch. When I started to open the door leading into the yard area, he asked, "Do you want me to try to wake Blaine? Maybe he's sobered up enough to drive you guys to your stands for the afternoon's hunt."

"No, no, Mr. Roy, that won't be necessary," I said. "Maybe he can sleep it off and at least have dinner with us when we get back tonight."

Mr. Roy then asked, "Are you sure? If Blaine wakes up and y'all are gone, he's going to be pissed."

"I can't help that, Mr. Roy. We'll see you at dark," I said.

I walked onto the front porch and saw Mike and Yeoman sitting in Blaine's truck with the air conditioning running full blast. I couldn't help noticing how fricking hot it was. I was shocked when I opened the driver's door and saw Yeoman sitting in the front seat wearing a T-shirt and shorts with his high-top snake boots. I couldn't hold back a chuckle as I said, "Damn, Yeoman, we're going hunting, not to the beach."

Yeoman responded, "Jack, I'm in a deer blind, and they can't see nothing except from the waist up. Besides, as you know, we haven't seen anything worth shooting anyway, so I might as well stay as cool as possible."

"Not a problem, Yeoman. Maybe it will change our luck," I said as we began our dusty drive into the scorching desert.

In just a few minutes, I completed the task of dropping off Yeoman and Mike. Then it took me only a few more minutes to get to my deer stand. I parked the truck in a group of mesquite trees, slowly gathered my gear, and walked to the deer stand. As I approached the ladder, I noticed there were no deer, hogs, or quail in sight. I thought it was too hot for the animals even to eat, much less stand in the middle of a *sandero* waiting on me to shoot them. I climbed the stairs of the stand. When I opened the door, a blast of stale heat just about sent me back down the ladder to the air-conditioned truck. As soon as I got inside, I opened all the windows, hoping I could catch a breeze. I thought, *I'll sure be glad when dark arrives. Maybe then it will cool down some.*

About twenty minutes before dark, I saw the same old group of wild hogs coming down the same *sandero*, sucking up every piece of corn they could find. It didn't take me a split second to decide I was going to shoot the biggest one in the group. The largest hog looked to be the size of a small cow and was black as the night on my farm. I thought it must be a sow and, as large as she was, the meat would feed a whole lot of Mr. Roy's folks in camp. Assuming that the South Texas

Hilton hunting camp would exist after we left.

When the group of hogs got closer, I slowly put my Remington Mag 7 out the window, getting ready for the kill. I had my big sow in the crosshairs of my scope and was looking for the exact spot to shoot her for a quick kill. I clicked the safety off, and then my Mag 7 was ready. When I began to squeeze the trigger, I could tell my breathing had gotten heavier. When I calmed myself, I continued to squeeze the trigger until the Mag 7 erupted with a loud crack. Wild hogs, including the one I shot at, ran in all directions into the desert brush and mesquite thickets. I thought I might shoot another one for the hell of it but quickly changed my mind. I thought, *How am I going to get this dead hog into the truck, much less two of them?*

I ignored Blaine's warning and got out of my stand to find the blood trail of the big sow. While I approached the area where my sow was supposed to be, I scanned the desert dirt for hog blood. It didn't take me long until I got to the exact spot where the hog was standing when I pulled the trigger. *What the hell? No blood!* I knew I was standing at the exact spot where I shot the big mama pig. *Just my luck, I missed.*

My daddy always said, "Son, I don't believe you could hit a bull in the ass with a silver spade."

I couldn't help wondering what else was going to go wrong before we got out of that godforsaken place. I loaded my gear into the back of the truck and headed to pick up Mike and Yeoman, who both reported they had not seen any deer big enough to shoot. On our brief ride back, we all complained about the desert heat and the lack of big bucks. Mike and Yeoman felt that, after the last two days of misery, they were more than ready to get back to North Carolina.

As we got closer, I saw the lights of the camp and the sparks of the mesquite wood burning in the fire pit. When we parked the truck, I saw Blaine sitting in one of the white plastic Walmart chairs with a drink in his hand.

"Thought I would sip on a short Jack Daniel's and Coke while waiting on you great North Carolina hunters to return," he said angrily.

Mike said to me in a low tone so Blaine wouldn't hear, "Looks like Blaine's still about half lit. No need to cause a ruckus, Jack. We're heading home tomorrow."

I decided that now was as good a time as any to tell

Blaine we were going home. I walked to Blaine's side and said, "It's hotter than hell down here, and there are no deer big enough to shoot. We decided that we're going to get out of your way and cut our trip short. We're headed home tomorrow." I stared into Blaine's bloodshot eyes and could tell he was terribly angry. "It's not your fault, Blaine. You have no control over the weather or the deer. There's no need for you to be pissed."

"Who said I'm pissed?" demanded Blaine. "Let's sit here and have a drink together while Mr. Roy cooks your steaks."

"Sure, Blaine, but I think I'll just have a cold bottle of water, if you don't mind," I said.

"Suit yourself," snapped Blaine.

Just then, Mr. Roy came to the fire pit with a platter of ribeye steaks. When each steak hit the fire grate, you could see and smell the sweet smoke of cooking steaks and burning mesquite wood.

While the steaks were cooking and the air was dead with silence, Yeoman tried to change the subject. "Let's talk about this Virginia turkey hunt you guys want to go on," he said.

"Well, Yeoman, my brother lives in Virginia, and he

sends me his copies of *Virginia Wildlife* magazine," I said. "I've never hunted turkeys, and I thought we might find a place to hunt there. Virginia won't be a long drive for us, and hunting turkeys in the spring should be a blast."

Mike said, "We probably could get on the web and find an outfitter in Virginia where we could book a spring turkey hunt."

Blaine was about three sheets to the wind when he spoke up: "Hey, I know a guy that owns over a thousand acres, and I bet I could get him to let y'all come hunt. Hey, he even has a hunting lodge for you to stay in and a base camp at the foot of the mountains. I go to his lodge every year to visit."

Trying to pacify Blaine, I answered, "That would be great. Thanks, Blaine."

Brian then spoke up and said, "I've never hunted turkeys. I read they're one of the hardest animals in the woods to shoot. I understand they can see you blink your eyes at a hundred yards, and hear you twice as far."

Blaine stumbled to his feet and said, "You're wrong, Brian. The hardest animal to hunt is a man." Everyone just looked at Blaine and wondered what he was going to say next. It didn't take long before Blaine picked up the remainder of the bottle of Jack and addressed the group. "You guys bore me. I think I'll seek my entertainment elsewhere. Good night." With that, Blaine and his bottle retired from the fire pit and headed toward his trailer.

Brian said, "Man, I'm glad he's gone. Tomorrow morning can't come fast enough."

"Hey, guys, I'm sorry. I promise I'll make it up to you," I said.

Before anyone could answer, Mr. Roy said, "Grab a plate and get your steak."

"Music to my ears, and stomach!" shouted Yeoman.

Mr. Roy woke us at five A.M., just like every morning we had been in camp.

I got up and dressed for the plane trip. I could hardly wait to get home and see Miss Bonnie. I guess I must had been a little slow that morning because, when I entered the mess hall, the rest of our group was already seated and eating breakfast. At the far end of the room, sitting all by himself, was Blaine. I wanted to talk to Blaine before I left, hoping I could smooth things over with him.

As I got closer to Blaine, I could see he was really hung over. The whites of his eyes looked like a red roadmap. I stopped and got a quick cup of coffee and then sat down with him. "Blaine, I'm sorry things didn't work out as planned," I said. "I hoped we could come down here and have a great time and hopefully kill a huge deer."

Blaine looked into my eyes and said, "No need to say another word. I am terribly ashamed of myself and how I've acted. The deer hunting was terrible, it was hot as hell, and then I stayed drunk the whole time you've been here. I'm so sorry I ruined your trip, and I need to make amends to all of you."

"No need, Blaine. We'll just chalk it up to history, and maybe someday we can look back at this fiasco and have a good laugh," I said.

"I don't think so," said Blaine. "I think that when you get your butt back to North Carolina, I won't ever talk to you or see you again. So I have to make it up to you, and here's my proposition, Listen up, all you knuckleheads!" Blaine stood up at his table and addressed the group. Everyone stopped eating and looked in his direction. I'm sure everyone wondered what he had to announce.

Blaine began, "I want to apologize for this terrible hunt and vacation you guys had here in Texas. I stayed drunk the entire time y'all been here. In addition to being drunk, my war demons returned and haunted me every day. I think I even told you a little about killing people during the Vietnam War. I told how I hunted them down and how hard some were to kill. For all this, I am extremely sorry and ashamed. I truly want to make this terrible hunt and my actions up to y'all. I remembered even in the fog of the alcohol that you guys want to go turkey hunting in Virginia. I've contacted my friend in Virginia and paid for an all-expenses turkey hunt for four. I booked it for the first week of April. It's the least I can do to make up for all your trouble, coming all the way down here for nothing."

Brian spoke first. "Man, that would be great, Blaine. And it was not really that bad."

"Oh, yes it was," countered Blaine. "I was an asshole, and I promise that I'll get myself back on the right track. Just as soon as you guys leave, I'm getting in my truck and driving back to Houston and checking myself in to an alcohol abuse and mental facility. I've paid for your hunt with my credit card, and you guys are all set to hunt turkeys in Virginia. I promise you'll have a great time and will limit out on turkeys at this great lodge. I wrote down all the important details and will give them to Jack before you guys leave."

I thought, *Yeah, right. When I get back to North Carolina and Miss Bonnie, I'm never going to think about or talk to him again.* Blaine had serious mental and emotional problems, and it was best that I distanced myself and my friends from this out-of-control guy.

Soon, the guys had loaded their gear into the same vehicles they rode in down to the South Texas Hilton.

When we got into the rental cars and were preparing to leave, Blaine approached my driver's-side window with a paper in his hand. I rolled down the window and said, "Blaine, I hope you beat this thing, and hopefully we'll be able to talk when you get yourself straight."

"I'll get back on the straight and narrow, I promise," said Blaine. "Wait, here is John's information for the turkey hunt in April." Blaine shoved the paper to me through the open window.

"Thanks. Blaine. We can hardly wait," I said. As I rolled up the window, I thought, *I've got to get out of here and out of his life.*

"Good luck, my old friend." Those were my last words to Blaine as I left him in Texas for what I hoped was forever. As we drove away, I looked back at Blaine and saw him waving goodbye as the Texas desert dust surrounded him.

CHAPTER SEVEN

We must have driven for at least an hour before anyone said anything.

Brian spoke first. "Man, I'll be so glad to get out of Texas. I can't wait to get back home. This trip has been exhausting, both physically and mentally."

"Guys, I'm sorry I brought y'all all the way down here for what was supposed to be the hunt of a lifetime, and all you got was a Texas hunt from hell," I said.

Brian quickly responded, "Hey, it's not your fault. Besides, we get an all-expenses-paid turkey hunt out of it, and I, for one, am excited."

Yeoman added, "Me, too. I'll have to see if my turkey-hunting vest and clothes still fit. I've gained a few pounds this year."

"I'm excited. I've read a lot about turkey hunting in Virginia," Mike said. "They have lots of turkeys, and hunting them in the mountains will certainly be a challenge."

Before I knew it, we were at the Corpus airport. We unloaded all our gear and checked it in for the flight. After the luggage was secured and we were headed for our gate, Yeoman looked at me and said, "No shenanigans on this flight, Rumsey."

"No problem, Yeoman. I just want to go to sleep on the plane and get home as soon as possible," I said.

Mike said, "Missing Miss Bonnie, are you, Jack?"

"Yeah, I can't wait to get home," I replied.

Brian added, "I can't wait for April to get here so we can shoot turkeys in Virginia. I bet that lodge and hunting land are beautiful. Wish we had pictures."

It seemed like it took forever for the plane to arrive back in Greensboro. When it finally landed, we retrieved and loaded our gear into JP's truck and headed home. I called Bonnie to let her know I landed safely and should be home within the hour.

When we pulled into my driveway, I saw Bonnie standing with the front door open, waiting anxiously for me. I got out of the truck and started to unload my hunting stuff. Bonnie motioned for me to leave it in the drive and get into the house. I left my rifle and all my gear in the driveway. Once inside, I got the biggest kiss and hug, as if I had been gone for years.

"Wow, maybe I should travel more often if I'm going to be welcomed like this every time I get home," I said.

"No more hunting trips for you," Bonnie replied. "I don't like being in this big house all alone. And besides, you just don't know how much I missed you."

"Let's get a cup of coffee and sit on the porch, and I'll tell you all about the worst hunting trip I've ever been on," I said.

After our coffee, Bonnie said, "Okay, let's hear all about this terrible hunt."

In detail, I told her about Blaine, his drinking, and how hot and miserable the deer hunting was. I told her the only thing I saw to shoot was a big, old sow hog and, hell, I even missed that. "Bonnie, that was the worst hunting trip I've ever been on," I said.

Bonnie replied, "Well, sounds like at least one thing went right."

"Really, what?" I asked.

"You, Yeoman, Mike, and Brian get to go turkey hunting in a few months," Bonnie said. "You and Mike have talked and read about turkey hunting in Virginia for several years. Now, it looks like y'all will be going in April, courtesy of Blaine."

"I don't know if I should go, especially if Blaine has anything to do with it," I said.

"You should go. It will be fun with Yeoman, Mike, and Brian staying in the lodge and at the base camp, not to mention the possibility of shooting a Virginia turkey," Bonnie said.

"Well, I'll think about it, but we have to get through winter first," I said.

The next week, I sold all my cows so I wouldn't have to feed hay all winter. At my age, it was hard enough to take my old bird dog, Sadie, for long walks every day. Going out in the cold, rain, and sometimes snow to feed cows hay was not something I cared to do. I just passed the winter days with Bonnie and the grandchildren and my old dog.

As each day passed, the daylight hours got shorter, and winter seemed to be getting longer. I tried to call all my hunting and beer-drinking buddies at least once a week to catch up on what was going on in their lives. Every time I spoke with Mike, Brian, and Yeoman, all they wanted to talk about was going turkey hunting that spring in Virginia. Yeoman especially liked the idea of a free hunt and going to the beautiful mountains of Virginia to eat the local foods.

Whenever he mentioned hunting in Virginia and all the food he wanted to try, I'd say, "Yeoman, you make it sound like we're going to another country. We're just going to travel to the next state."

Yeoman would reply, "Maybe not another country, but at least in Virginia we can get homemade apple butter. That's something you can't get around Davie County."

"Yeah, I can't remember the last time I ate hot Southern biscuits dripping with fresh apple butter," I replied.

One day when Sadie and I returned from our long walk around the farm, I noticed that Bonnie's star magnolia had begun to bloom. A star magnolia is a slow-growing tree or bush native to Japan. It has large, snowy flowers and blooms in the very early spring, usually around the last week of February. The star magnolia even blooms before it sprouts its leaves. A few years earlier, Bonnie had asked me to plant a star magnolia in remembrance of her mother, Dessie, who had passed. Bonnie's mother was the sweetest mother-in-law any man could ask for. I loved her very much and missed her almost as much as Bonnie did.

In what seemed like a flash, March was here. Folks around our little farm were planting gardens, fertilizing yards and pastures, and getting ready for Easter. Every day, I got a call from Mike, Yeoman, or Brian to make sure I was still going hunting in Virginia. I told Bonnie I thought I would go with the guys and hopefully have some fun and learn more about turkey hunting. Heck, I might even be able to bag a bird for Thanksgiving.

Bonnie said, "If you guys are going to Virginia in April, don't you think you should contact Blaine's guy to make sure you're still on for this hunt?"

"Great idea. I'll call him right now," I said.

I took the house phone onto the porch and dialed the number written on the crumpled piece of paper Blaine had shoved in my hand when I left the ranch in Texas. The phone rang only once, as if John were sitting and waiting on my call.

"John Drain here," he said.

"Mr. Drain, my name is Jack Rumsey, and a mutual friend of ours gave me your name and number to call regarding the possibility of turkey hunting on your place this spring," I said.

"Well, first of all, my name is John. Mr. Drain was my father. I've been expecting your call," he said. "Blaine said that you and your group are the nicest bunch of guys to have hunting on my property. Blaine paid me quite a sum of money for your hunt and your stay at my lodge in April. The season comes in on April 13, and I've got everything all ready for you guys. I've put out lots of trail cameras, and I can tell you we have a record number of turkeys this spring on my place. Y'all will have a blast. Now, let's see. There are four of you coming to hunt in April, is that right?"

"Yes, four of us will arrive on April 12 and hunt Saturday the thirteenth, Sunday the fourteenth, and Monday the fifteenth, then return to North Carolina on the sixteenth," I said.

John replied, "Perfect. I'll email you instructions on what to bring on your hunt, as well as the address for the lodge. Your GPS should bring you right to the front door of my lodge. You have my number if you have any questions before you head this way. We're looking forward to your arrival in Virginia," he added.

"We?" I asked.

"Oh, I forgot to mention my son, who helps me take care of the hunters and the lodge. My son's name is Todd. Todd is thirty years old and is somewhat physically and mentally challenged. Todd can't speak or do physically what most men can, but he's the best son and friend a dad could ask for," John said proudly.

"I'm looking forward to meeting you and Todd. We're getting excited about our turkey hunt," I said.

A few minutes later, I heard a ping on my iPhone,

indicating I had received an email. I took a glance at my phone and saw that John had done as promised and emailed me an attachment with his address and instructions on what to do to prepare before coming to Virginia. Immediately after I read his email, I called Mike, Brian, and my old friend Yeoman, letting them know about my conversation with John.

When I talked to Mike, he said, "I'll call everybody and arrange for us to meet at your shed tomorrow and make plans for our turkey trip. I'm so excited. If you could get Miss Bonnie to make some Redneck Caviar, I'll have Brian get the chips and beer. I'll bring some turkey-hunting shows I recorded off the Outdoor Channel."

I asked, "The Outdoor Channel? What shows?"

Mike responded, "I've filmed every turkey-hunting show the legends have done. Harold Knight and David Hale. They're the best in the business, and you can learn a lot by just watching their TV shows."

"Great. I'm sure Bonnie won't mind, and thanks for bringing the videos. I need all the help I can get," I said. "See you guys tomorrow afternoon."

I got up early the next morning in anticipation of the guys coming over. I grabbed a quick cup of coffee and shoved down a bowl of corn flakes. When I finished my breakfast, I decided to make Bonnie a fresh cup of coffee and surprise her with a Danish as well. I put Bonnie's breakfast on a tray and took it to her while she was still in bed.

She woke up and was surprised to see me up so early. "What a pleasant surprise, and it's not even my birthday," Bonnie said. "Okay, what do you want?"

"I wanted to let you know that the guys are coming over later to talk about our upcoming hunting trip to Virginia," I said. "Would you make Redneck Caviar for me and the guys? You don't mind, do you?"

"Of course, I don't mind," Bonnie responded.

"Mike is going to bring turkey-hunting videos for us to watch, so I can try to figure out how to hunt these birds," I said.

"Okay, you better get The Shed cleaned up and make sure the DVR is working," Bonnie said.

I leaned over, gave her a big kiss, and said, "Love you, honey. You are the best."

"Yes, I know, and I love you, too," Bonnie whispered.

With that, I blew her a kiss as I closed our bedroom door and headed for my shed.

CHAPTER EIGHT

The day passed quickly. I cleaned up The Shed and got the DVR ready for my first lesson on the art of turkey hunting.

Mike was the first to arrive, with Yeoman riding shotgun in Mike's F-150 pickup. Yeoman slowly but surely climbed out of Mike's truck and headed for The Shed. "You need to get me a stool so I can get in and out of that truck, Mike," said Yeoman. "I'm too short and fat to climb that high, not to mention too old."

Yeoman was still fussing about the truck when I saw Brian driving down my driveway, headed for The Shed.

"Sorry I'm late," said Brian as he opened the truck door.

"Right on time. Besides, Yeoman's not through fussing about Mike's truck," I said.

"Sorry, guys, I'm just hungry," said Yeoman. "Y'all know how grumpy I get when I'm hungry. Has Bonnie got that redneck stuff ready?"

Everyone laughed as I walked over to the fridge and got the bowl of caviar. Yeoman opened a big bag of Tostitos chips while Mike loaded the first Knight and Hale's *Ultimate Hunting* video in the DVR and Brian got beer for everyone.

"All right, guys, settle down. This is serious business. Y'all need to be paying attention, especially Jack," Mike said.

After watching just a few minutes of the first show, I realized there was a lot more to turkey hunting than I thought. I had thought it would be fairly easy, but no.

After three or four videos, Mike cut off the TV and told everyone to listen up. "Okay, here's the long and short of it," he said. "You see, hunting turkeys is so difficult because you're trying to reverse nature."

"What are you talking about, Mike?" I asked.

"Turkeys roost high in the trees at night, and as morning

begins to break and the songbirds begin to sing, the male turkey, or gobbler, does two things," said Mike. "The gobbler is very protective of his hens, and he lets the world know that he's the boss of the woods. When the crow calls or the owl hoots, lots of times the gobbler will gobble at their calls, saying, 'Hey, I'm the boss in these woods.' While on roost, a gobbler sits high on his tree limb and gobbles to tell all his lady friends, 'Hey, I'm over here. You need to come to me to breed.' That's why they're so hard to kill, because in nature the hen goes to the gobbler to get bred. So we're trying to reverse nature by having the gobbler come to us. Usually, this is very difficult, especially when the gobbler already has lots of hens around. Another way to locate a gobbler is when an owl or crow calls and the turkey gobbles. When the turkey gobbles at an owl or crow call, lots of times you can locate exactly where he is. I brought each of you a crow call and an owl call to practice with. Early in the morning, when the woods begin to wake and the birds begin to sing, you should blow on one of these calls to get the gobbler to reveal his location by gobbling. It's called 'shock calling.' Here, try this owl call, Jack."

I picked up the call, put it to my lips, and blew, but no sound.

"Wrong end. What an idiot," laughed Yeoman.

I turned the owl call around, and Mike said, "While you blow on the call, try to blow the sound of 'Who cooks for you, who cooks for you-all.' When done right, it will sound just like a hoot owl, thereby hopefully making the gobbler gobble."

" 'Who cooks for you, who cooks for you-all,' " I blew. It sounded like a sick owl. "Guess I need a lot of practice," I said.

"Good thing we have ten days before we leave for Virginia," Brian said.

Mike continued, "Okay, once you locate where the gobbler has roosted, then you move through the woods, getting as close to the gobbler as you can without spooking him. Once you get as close as you can, find a good place to set up to call to the gobbler."

"Who wants another beer?" Brian asked, then continued, "Once you get set up, what do you do to get the gobbler to come to you?"

Mike said, "I thought you'd never ask. After it's full daylight and the turkeys have flown off roost, you need to softly call on a friction call to hopefully get the gobbler into shooting range. Here's a friction call. It's used to sound like a hen calling. You can yelp, purr, or cackle by using this call."

"Okay, let me get this straight. So I want to sound like a hen so the gobbler will come to me, thinking he's going to breed, and I shoot him right in the face," I joked.

"Yep, that's it," Mike said.

"Imagine you're the gobbler's girlfriend, and you sweet-talk him by using this call," said Yeoman. "So you basically are saying, 'Hey, big boy, come over here and see what I have waiting for you.' "

"The gobbler comes over thinking he's going to get lucky, and *boom*, he's dead," said Mike.

Yeoman said, "Sex is a powerful attracting tool even with turkeys. Just like when the buck deer chase the does looking to breed and do foolish things and get shot for all their efforts."

Mike added, "When the turkey is pissed off, his head turns red. And when he is feeding or just chilling, his head is blue. But when he thinks he's going to get lucky with a hen, his head turns white."

"So, when you think the turkey is coming to you, be looking for a white head coming through the woods," added Yeoman. "When the turkey is within about forty-five yards, slowly raise your gun and shoot him only in the head."

"Why only in the head?" I asked.

Mike spoke up. "Several reasons. First, you want him to die right where you shot him. Second, if you shoot him other than in the head, he'll run off and die, and you just lost your trophy."

Brian said, "Hey, guys, it's been fun, but I have to run. I promised my wife we'd go out to eat supper, and I'm late."

Mike, Yeoman, and Brian got up from their chairs and headed toward the door. Mike turned to me and said, "Make sure you watch all the videos and practice your calling."

Over the next few days, I continued to watch Harold Knight and David Hale's *Ultimate Hunting* videos, trying to learn as much as I could about turkey hunting. The more shows I watched, the more doubts I had that I would be successful. I thought, *Even if I don't shoot a turkey, at least I'll be able to spend some time in the beautiful woods of Virginia with my good friends.*

Soon, it was the day before our trip. Yeoman called me at least five times, making sure I had packed all the right gear for my first turkey-hunting trip. "Make sure you have your gloves, face mask, camo T-shirt, camo regular shirt, camo pants, camo muck boots, and, finally, your turkey vest," said Yeoman. "Make sure your turkey vest has your owl call, crow call, and mouth and friction calls for the hunt. Oh, and don't forget your gun and shells."

Yeoman and Mike were the only ones of the four of us who had ever hunted turkeys, much less killed one. Brian and I had high hopes of at least seeing and hearing some big gobblers. Just experiencing the thrill of the hunt would be icing on the cake. It really didn't matter if we killed anything. Just spending time in God's creation with good friends would be enough for all of us.

Bonnie came into the bedroom, where I had laid out all the hunting clothes I owned. "Time to pack, sweetheart," I said.

Bonnie always hated to see me go out of town, even

for just a few days. "I know I encouraged you to go turkey hunting with the guys, but I wish you would sit this trip out. For some reason, I have a bad feeling about it," she said.

"Oh, you say that about every trip, Bonnie," I said.

"Yes, I know, but this one is different somehow," said Bonnie. "I have a really terrible feeling that something bad is going to happen."

"Everything is going to be just fine. And besides, I'll only be gone for four days. I'll be back before you know I'm gone," I said, trying to reassure her.

"Okay, if you must. Let's get you packed so we can spend some time together before you have to leave in the morning," said Bonnie.

The evening wore on, and we went to bed early, hoping for a good night's sleep before the trip to Virginia.

The next morning, Bonnie and I had our second cup of coffee while sitting in the den waiting on the guys to arrive. We talked about being careful and the need for me to call at least two times a day.

"Bonnie, John said there's a good cell signal at the lodge but no cell service at the base camp, and certainly not on the mountain where I'll be hunting," I said. "Just know I'll call whenever possible to let you know I'm fine and everything is okay. Hopefully, I'll call to report that each of us has killed a turkey and we'll be coming home early."

"I don't care about a stupid turkey. I just want you home," Bonnie said.

Just then, Mike blew the horn of his F-150 to let me know he was in the driveway waiting on me. I grabbed my hunting bag and headed for the front door with Bonnie close at my heels.

"Jack, please don't go," Bonnie begged. "Something terrible is going to happen, I just know it. I'm scared."

"Everything is going to be just fine. Now, give me a big kiss, and I'll see you in a few days," I said.

Mike and Brian jumped out of the truck the moment I opened the front door. Brian was the first to come to the porch to help with my hunting bag. While Brian loaded my gear into the truck, Mike told Bonnie not to worry, that we would be back before she knew it.

"Mike, please, y'all be careful," said Bonnie. "I have a terrible feeling that something awful is going to happen."

Mike said, "Now, Bonnie, you know I'm not going to let anything happen to your sweetie. See you soon."

I turned to Bonnie and gave her a big hug and kiss and told her not to worry and that I would call when we got there.

Yeoman was sitting in the front seat of the truck watching all the goodbyes and the loading of the gear. When I got settled in the backseat and Mike was backing out of the drive, Yeoman said, "You and Bonnie make me sick. All that lovey-dovey stuff."

"Yeoman, you're just jealous," I said.

Brian said, "How long a drive do we have before we get to the lodge?"

Mike said, "The GPS says five hours and we should be there."

Yeoman said, "I'm starving." He pulled a grocery bag from under his seat and began to remove all kinds of candy bars, bags and bags of chips, three cans of Beanee Weenee, a pack of saltine crackers, and a six-pack of Diet Coke.

"Hand me a bag of chips, Yeoman," said Mike.

"No way, Mike. You should have packed your own snacks. Besides, there's only enough for me," said Yeoman.

I looked over at Brian, and he was already napping. I thought that was a pretty good idea—should make the trip faster. For the next few hours, I drifted in and out of sleep as we traveled to my first turkey hunt in Virginia.

Mike said, "Hey, Jack and Brian, wake up. We're stopping for lunch. Where do you guys want to eat?"

Yeoman answered, "Kentucky Fried Chicken is great for me. That way, I can get a bucket of chicken and a small dessert to hold me until dinner."

"That's twelve pieces of chicken, mashed potatoes, slaw, and biscuits. Are you kidding me?" I said.

"Don't forget the dessert," said Yeoman.

We all just laughed as we pulled into the parking lot of the Kentucky Fried Chicken.

THE TURKEY KILLER: A Novel by JACK SNOW

CHAPTER NINE

Soon after lunch, we were on John's drive, heading to his home and the hunting lodge. John had a driveway that was at least five miles of gravel, lined on each side with blooming apple trees. In just a few minutes, we saw an old, two-story white farmhouse with a log hunting lodge next to it. When we got closer, we saw a man who looked about our age sitting on the front porch of the old farm home. The gentleman was quick to move from the porch and meet our truck at the end of the driveway.

"Hi, I'm John Drain," he said. "Welcome to my home and hunting lodge."

We got out of the truck and stretched our legs after being cramped up in Mike's pickup.

"Hey, John. I'm Jack Rumsey. We spoke on the phone just the other day," I said while I shook John's hand. "I'd like you to meet my good friends Mike, Brian, and big Yeoman."

"It sure is nice to finally meet you guys. It seems like I already know you after talking to Blaine so many times," said John. "I talked to Blaine just yesterday. He wanted to make sure you guys were coming, and that everything was all set for your hunt."

I thought it was odd that Blaine called to check on us, but then I guess he just wanted to make sure all was well.

"Let me show you around the lodge, and then we can visit the base camp," said John. "Once we get to the base camp, we can discuss who will be hunting on which of the four mountains."

When we entered the front door of the log lodge, we walked into a big den with a kitchen and breakfast room attached. The den had a huge rock fireplace with a slate hearth. An old log was used for the mantel above. The den floors were crafted out of rough wood, as was the paneling surrounding the room. Several deer and turkey mounts were placed along the walls. Most all the deer mounts were of record deer; one had as many as fourteen points. There were also lots of turkey mounts, most of them gobblers with long, thick beards and long spurs.

"The lodge is beautiful, John. You must be very proud," Mike said.

"This old lodge was built by my father years ago," said John. "Just in the past ten years or so, Todd and I have turned it into a hunting camp serving both deer and turkey hunters. We sell three- and four-day hunts that include lodging, as well as some of the best Southern food you'll find in the whole state. There are four bedrooms, each with its own bath. So just pick a room and put your bags up, and we'll take a quick ride to the base camp, where you'll spend the night after each hunt—that is, unless you kill a turkey. When you're successful and kill your gobbler, you'll return here, visit, and eat while waiting on everyone to return to the lodge."

Yeoman spoke first. "Okay, John, so we spend the night here, and then in the morning we travel to the base camp and begin turkey hunting, right?"

Mike was quick to add, "Once we begin hunting, when we kill our turkey, then we come back to the lodge and wait until all return."

"That's about it," said John. "Now, pick a bedroom, put your gear up, and we'll each take a Polaris Ranger so I can show you the way to the base camp."

Just then, a young man came in the back door of the lodge holding a handful of eggs. John quickly said, "This is my son, Todd. Todd doesn't talk, nor can he do a lot of physical work, but he's a great hand around the lodge and isn't a bad cook either."

Todd looked to be in his late twenties or early thirties. He was very pale in complexion and quite tall and skinny. He had blond hair and lots of freckles and wore a huge, wide smile on his young face. Each of us shook Todd's hand as we told him our names. Todd reacted by smiling from ear to ear.

"Okay, guys, I got four Polaris UTVs out in the backyard. Let's take a quick ride to the base camp," said John. We walked to our camo Rangers, and John got into the passenger side of my vehicle. "Just follow the path at the end of my driveway. It's only about four miles to the base camp."

As we were driving, John talked about how long he had owned the farm and lodge and how he loved what he did for a living. I thought now was a good time to ask John how he knew Blaine. John told me he and Blaine were old buddies from Vietnam. He also said he and Blaine had kept in touch throughout the years, and that Blaine came to his lodge every year to hunt deer and visit. He went on to tell me that both he and Blaine went through hell during the war, and that it had taken him years to forget all he had seen and done during the conflict.

Soon, we arrived at the base camp, which was identical to the hunting lodge except much smaller. I remembered that I needed to call Bonnie to tell her that we had gotten here and all was well. When I took my phone out of my pocket, John said, "No use trying to call anyone from here. There's no cell signal. But you can call when we get back to the lodge." John then added, "This will be your new home beginning in the morning, unless you kill your trophy turkey. Now, let's get back to the lodge. I'm sure Todd already has supper cooking."

"Music to my ears. I'm starving," said Yeoman.

Mike interrupted, "John, I thought we were going to

decide which mountain we're to hunt."

"You're correct, Mike, but we're running short on time, and we don't want to be late for Todd's supper," said John. "No worries. When we get back to the lodge, we'll discuss who'll be hunting where."

We all got into our respective Rangers, John riding with me again, and headed back to the hunting lodge. There was little talk between John and me. It seemed that John had a lot on his mind and really didn't want to talk. I thought it was odd that he didn't ask any questions regarding his new guests. I thought he might inquire about where we were from, our turkey-hunting abilities, and what we did for a living.

John finally broke the silence and said, "Let's hurry back to the lodge. Todd will have supper ready, and he'll be pissed if we're late."

Soon, we arrived back at the lodge and parked our Rangers in the front yard beside Mike's truck. Yeoman, Mike, Brian, and I stopped on the front porch to sit and relax before supper. John never spoke. He just rushed through the front door while yelling his son's name.

Mike asked the obvious question: "Did we do something

to piss John off, or is he just that way?"

Brian said, "Well, you have to think this is just a job for him. Same old stuff every day."

"Yes, but if you want repeat business, you'd think he'd be a little more attentive to us and our needs," said Yeoman.

"Like how?" asked Brian.

"Well, he should have had snacks and cold beer waiting on the front porch when we returned from the base camp," said Yeoman. "Like chicken fingers, dips, chips, and boiled shrimp, maybe even some Redneck Caviar."

Mike looked at him and said, "All you ever talk about is eating, Yeoman. And besides, John and Todd probably don't even know what Redneck Caviar is."

Just then, the front door opened, and John came onto the porch and said, "Supper is ready, and we should not keep Todd waiting. He gets angry and agitated when his hard work gets cold." He added, "Please, whether you like the food or not, make sure you tell Todd how great his meal was, and that it was the best you have ever eaten. Trust me, you don't want to make Todd mad."

Yeoman said, "Okay, we got it. What's for supper, John?"

John said, "Todd has made his favorite meal—fried chicken, baked pork chops, turnip greens, black-eyed peas, and mashed potatoes with cornbread and sweet tea."

John then opened the screen door of the lodge. Yeoman was the first to head to the dining area, followed by Mike and Brian.

I stayed on the porch and asked John if we have done anything to upset him.

"What do you mean?" said John.

"Well, you're not very talkative," I said. "I thought we may have done something to upset you."

"Not at all," said John. "I get nervous when we have new guests at camp, and I just have a lot on my mind. I want to make sure y'all have a great time."

"John, don't worry about us. We enjoy just being together, and it don't matter if we kill a turkey or not. We just like hunting together, visiting with each other, and making memories," I said.

John then opened the screen door and said, "Now, let's eat."

"I'm going to call Bonnie, and then I'll be on in," I said.

"Remember what I said about Todd getting upset. Don't be long," warned John.

I looked at my cell phone and saw that I had a strong signal. I hit the Bonnie icon on speed dial. In just seconds, I heard Bonnie's sweet voice.

"I was getting worried," she said. "It's after six and you hadn't called yet."

"Bonnie, I'm sorry, but we've been real busy unpacking and visiting the base camp," I said. "I tried to call from the base camp, but there was no signal. In fact, sweetheart, there's not a signal anywhere in these mountains except here at the lodge. Well, Bonnie, I have to go. Supper is ready, and John says I don't want to make the cook mad by not being on time."

Bonnie just laughed and said, "You're kidding, right?"

"No, I'm serious. John said Todd gets really mad if anything goes wrong with his cooking, and that also means we have to be on time and praise everything Todd does," I said.

"Sounds like you're going to have a great time," Bonnie said in a sarcastic tone. "I told you I had a bad feeling about this hunting trip. Okay, guess you should go. Don't want to make the cook mad. Remember to be safe, and I love you."

"I love you and will call when I can, sweetheart. Good night," I said.

I opened the wide screen door and entered the lodge to see that Yeoman, Mike, and Brian had fixed their plates and were eating at the big wooden dining table.

Yeoman said, "Jack, this food is great, especially the fried chicken. You need to grab your plate before I eat it all."

I walked into the kitchen and could tell that Todd was pissed by the look on his face. "Sorry I'm a little late, Todd. I had to call home," I said.

Todd turned and looked me straight in the eye and shoved a plate into my stomach. I guess that was his way of saying, *Don't be late again or else.* I took my plate and filled it with pork chops, mashed potatoes, turnip greens, black-eyed peas, and a large piece of cornbread. I could tell this hunt was going to be a challenge, but at least beginning tomorrow morning we would be alone at the base camp, away from John and Todd, at least until we killed our turkeys. The rule was that we had to return from the base camp to the hunting lodge once we tagged our turkeys. I guess they did that so they wouldn't have to store so many supplies at the base camp.

Mike said, "What was that all about with you and Todd?"

"Guess he didn't like me calling Bonnie and being late for supper," I said.

Just as soon as we finished our last bite, John said, "Okay, guys, follow me and we'll determine who will be hunting where in the morning. I meant to show you where to hunt tomorrow while at the base camp, but we just didn't have time. Good thing I have a full map of each mountain here in the lodge."

I said, "Shouldn't we help clean up our plates first, John?"

"No," John said sternly. "Todd doesn't like anyone messing with his job."

"No problem," I whispered as I followed everyone into the main living room.

When we entered, I saw that John had taken out a huge map of the property and put it on a large coffee table in the middle of the room. He pointed to the map and said, "Okay, guys, here on the map I've labeled the base camp and the roads leading from the backyard to each of the four mountains you'll be hunting on. Brian will be on mountain #1, Mike on #2, Yeoman on mountain #3, and, finally, Jack on #4. I'll wake y'all in the morning at four-thirty, and Todd will have breakfast ready. After breakfast, y'all will load your hunting gear, get into your Rangers, and proceed to the base camp. When it begins to get daylight, each will go to the top of your respective mountain and begin hunting. Should you kill a turkey, stop back at the base camp, gather up your hunting gear, bring your turkey back to the lodge, and Todd will dress your bird. Any questions?"

Mike spoke first. "No, John, I think we got it."

Brian said, "Yep, this is not our first rodeo."

"Wait, I have a question," I said. "Let's say that on the first day, Yeoman kills a turkey, and he returns to the lodge. Does that mean the next day one of us can hunt on the mountain Yeoman was on?"

John looked at the group and said, "Let me be perfectly clear. You can hunt only on your assigned mountain and can't switch hunting areas for any reason. It is extremely important that we know exactly where each of you are hunting, just in case you get lost. Remember, there is no cell signal on the mountains."

I thought, *This is really weird, but rules are rules, whatever the reason.* "Okay, got it, John," I said.

"Just one more detail. Do not cross the top of your assigned mountain onto the other side," instructed John. "That is national game land, and there will probably be other hunters there. If you happen to see someone hunting on your side of the mountain, tell them they should go back across the mountain to the national game land."

"Okay, John, we got it. I'm sure I'll be back here tomorrow night with my turkey, enjoying Todd's supper," Mike boasted. "John, you want to join us on the porch for a cold beer before bed?"

"No thanks," John replied. "Todd and I will be turning in now, and I suggest you guys do the same, as four-thirty comes very early in these hills."

Yeoman said, "Well, I, for one, can't sleep without at least one cold beer."

As John and Todd walked toward the back door of the lodge, John turned toward Yeoman and said, "Suit yourself."

Mike opened the big Yeti cooler we had brought from my

shed, grabbed four beers, and said to the rest of us, "See you on the porch."

We each grabbed a rocking chair on the front porch and opened a long-awaited cold beer. When John and Todd were completely out of sight, I said, "Man, is this crazy or what?"

Brian said, "Well, it's all free, so let's just have a good time."

"Yeah, Jack, don't get your panties in a wad. They just have their way of doing stuff," Yeoman said, then added, "I wonder if there's any fried chicken left for a night snack."

"Dang, Yeoman, you just ate. You can't be hungry," Mike said. Everyone just laughed because we knew Yeoman was dead serious about the snack.

We finished our beers and headed to our respective bedrooms. "See you in the morning, guys," I said as I closed my door.

It was only nine o'clock and I couldn't sleep, so I decided to call Bonnie and wish her good night. The phone rang four times, but she didn't answer. When I returned my phone to the charger, it began to ring.

"Sorry I couldn't get to the phone. I was getting ready for

bed," said Bonnie. "I thought you'd be asleep by now."

"I couldn't go to sleep thinking about you, and I'm a little apprehensive about hunting tomorrow," I said.

"Don't worry. I know you've never hunted turkeys before, but you'll do just fine," said Bonnie.

"It's not that, Bonnie. This place just seems weird with all of John's rules, not to mention you have to tiptoe around his son, Todd. If you're not there at the exact moment when it's time to eat, Todd gets pissed, and the rules for hunting are pretty demanding as well. We can't hunt together, we can't hunt on each other's mountain, and when you kill your turkey you have to load up your gear and return to the lodge. Please remind me never to come back up here to hunt again. I'll just hunt around the house from now on. At least that way, I'll be there with you at night instead of sleeping in a lodge listening to Yeoman snoring three doors down, not to mention having to stay in a lodge with an old man and his crazy son."

Bonnie laughed and said, "I guess that was why I felt uneasy about this hunt. Now, you need to get some sleep."

"You're right. I love you, and I'll call again when I get

back to the lodge. Remember, I'll be home in four days," I said as I put down my phone.

Just then, I remembered that I had packed a pair of earplugs in my bag just for this occasion. I retrieved them from my suitcase and thought, *Let it rip, Yeoman. You're not going to bother me.*

CHAPTER TEN

The next thing I remembered was John banging on my bedroom door and yelling, "It's four-thirty, and Todd has breakfast ready. Let's go!"

I jumped up and went to the restroom to wash up and get dressed for my first day of turkey hunting.

Before I got my boots on, John was back at my door, shouting, "Let's go, Todd is waiting!"

I opened the door and headed to the dining area, where I saw all three of my buddies eating a huge breakfast of country ham, grits, gravy, eggs, and hot biscuits.

Mike was the first to speak. "Good morning. You won the

prize for pissing Todd off again this morning."

John yelled from the kitchen, "Hurry and eat! I've got all the Rangers running and ready to go."

I gulped down a cup of warm black coffee and ate a biscuit filled with ham and eggs.

Yeoman said, "Jack, I got your stuff and loaded it into your Ranger to save time."

"Thanks, Yeoman," I said as I walked out the screen door into the dark morning, looking for my Ranger.

Just that quick, we were each driving down the long dirt road on our way to the base camp at the foot of the four mountains we were to hunt. During the cool, dark ride, I thought, *I'm not very impressed with this hunting lodge. Maybe all of us will kill a turkey the first day, and we can return to the lodge and back home the next morning.* Thinking about Bonnie, I wished I had taken her advice and stayed home. *Oh, well, I'm here now, and I should just make the most of it,* I thought. *At least we'll have something to reminisce and joke about when we sit around the campfire at my shed.*

Soon, I saw the streetlight in the backyard of the base camp. All four Rangers were in a dusty straight line, headed for the light. Just beyond the streetlight, I saw a post with signs numbering each of the four roads that led up the mountains we were to hunt on.

When we stopped and got out of our Rangers, Mike said, "It will be at least fifteen minutes before it's light enough for us to drive to the tops of the mountains to begin hunting."

"Why do we need to wait for more light to drive?" I asked. "My Ranger has headlights."

Looking frustrated, Mike said, "I can tell this is your first turkey hunt. The headlights of your Ranger would scare every turkey off your mountain. In a few minutes, it will be light enough for us to follow the roads to the tops of the mountains but dark enough for the turkeys to still be on roost."

"Oh, I would never have thought about that," I said.

Mike added, "When you get to your hunting spot and the songbirds start to sing, remember to use you owl call to make the turkey gobble on roost."

"Got it, brother. Just like I watched Harold Knight and David Hale use an owl call on video several times," I said.

"Maybe you'll have beginner's luck and your turkeys will

gobble on their own," Yeoman added.

Brian then said, "While I'm under this streetlight, I'm going to go ahead and put on my face mask and gloves." Each of us reached into our turkey-hunting vest and retrieved our gloves and face mask. While we were putting them on, Brian said, "Good luck, guys. I'm out of here. I got a big, old gobbler waiting on me."

With that, we got into our Rangers and began to drive up our assigned mountains.

When I got to the top of my mountain, I saw that John had placed a sign that said, "Park here." *Leave it to John*, I thought. I turned off my Ranger and began looking for a clear path into the woods. It was still dark as hell, and I finally realized I didn't know where I was or what I was doing. I was, however, not going to give up. I walked into the woods about two hundred yards from the Ranger and began looking for a place to sit and wait for daybreak. At the very top of the mountain, I finally found a large tree with a huge base. I placed my turkey-hunting stool at the base, sat down, and tried to get comfortable. I was also hoping the brief rest would settle my nerves. To be honest, it was a little scary to sit on top of the mountain, all alone and in the dark. I held my gun tight and waited.

Soon, it began to get lighter, and the mountain came alive with the sounds of redbirds, wrens, and other songbirds. I thought about all the videos by Harold and David. I remembered that now was the time to try to shock-gobble a turkey by using my owl call. I thought that once I used the call, one of two things was going to happen. I was either going to shock a gobbler into gobbling or, because I was terrible at owl calling, I was going to scare all my turkeys to other mountains.

I looked through my vest and finally found the owl call Mike had given me. When I raised it to my lips and began to use the call, I heard a loud, terrible owl call within probably fifty yards of where I sat. I thought that someone else must be hunting on my mountain, because his call sounded worse than mine. Following the blast of the sick owl call, gobblers sounded off. I heard *Gobble, gobble*, then another *Gobble*, all within a hundred yards of where I sat. The hair stood up on the back of my neck for two reasons. First, I had three gobblers within a hundred yards. Second, another hunter must have crossed from the national game land and was now hunting within fifty yards of me. I strained my eyes, looking for someone where I thought the owl call came from, but it was still too dark, and the underbrush was too thick. Then another terrible owl call came, this time farther away than the first but from the same direction. All three gobblers sounded off again. I thought maybe it was just a sick owl whose call sounded worse than mine. Or if it was another hunter, maybe he realized he needed to get back to the national game land on the other side of the mountain and was headed in that direction.

I immediately turned my attention to the gobbling turkeys and away from the sick owl or other hunter. When daylight turned to early morning, hens began yelping and clucking in the nearby trees. Every time a hen yelped or clucked, the gobblers sounded off, sometimes gobbling three or four times in a row. I was so excited I could barely sit still, and I strained my eyes looking for roosting turkeys.

Soon, I heard my first roosting turkey fly down from its high perch in the nearby hardwood trees. The sound was really loud, as if it were tearing down the forest with each leap from its roosting place. Soon, more and more turkeys were flying down to the ground. A few hens cackled when they hit the ground, which caused the gobblers to go crazy with gobbles. I was really pumped, and I had not even touched any of my calls. *Maybe I'll kill a big gobbler without having to use one of Mike's Knight and Hale game calls*, I thought. Then, all of a sudden, the woods became deathly quiet. No more gobbling, no hens cackling or yelping, just me and the mountain trees and the songbirds. I was puzzled until I remembered that on one of Harold and David's turkey shows, David had the same experience. He explained that when the turkeys gobbled, the hens would fly to them to breed. And if the gobblers were surrounded by hens, they had no need to gobble because they had all the women they wanted. David said that in this situation, about the only thing you could do was to sit still and use your best hen call to let the gobblers know where you were. That way, when all the hens were bred, the gobbler would remember where you were and come looking for you.

I looked in my vest for the Old Yeller friction call Mike had given me and prepared to make my first hen yelp. The woods were extremely quiet as I brought the wooden striker across the top half of the call, making what I thought was a great-sounding hen yelp. *Gobble, gobble* blasted from no more than ten yards behind me. It scared me so badly I threw my call, striker, and gun into the air and halfway down the mountain. The gobbler that had slipped up behind me took off like a jet. When it flew, it seemed like the ground exploded, and the trees sounded like a chainsaw was cutting down everything in the turkey's path. Within my first hour of turkey hunting, I had managed to scare every animal on that mountain, including all the turkeys.

The rest of my day passed without seeing or hearing any turkeys. I used the time to practice my turkey-calling skills on friction calls, box calls, and even my mouth calls. When the sun began to set, I was glad to walk back to the Ranger for my peaceful ride back down the mountain to the base camp. The Ranger fired up with the first twist of the key, and I just sat there and watched the mountain go to sleep and wished I could call Bonnie.

Slowly, I drove down the dirt road to the base camp. When I got close, I saw Mike and Yeoman standing in the backyard by their Rangers.

When I pulled up next to the guys, I asked, "Where's Brian?"

Mike said, "He killed a turkey and is back at the hunting lodge enjoying a great supper."

"He left a note on the kitchen table that said he shot a huge turkey and will see us in a couple of days," Yeoman explained.

Mike said, "I heard a gunshot about ten this morning that came from the direction where Brian was hunting. I bet he was back at the lodge by lunch."

"Good for Brian. Now, let's get in the cabin and fix something for supper," I said.

Yeoman added, "Yeah, I'm starved. I only packed four sandwiches, and they were all gone by noon."

The three of us went into the cabin and began to put away our hunting gear. Afterward, I went into the kitchen and started to gather all the stuff I needed to make tacos for supper. For fixing breakfast and supper, the kitchen had a pantry loaded with soups, crackers, bread, pancake mixes, and several taco kits. In the fridge were several fresh hamburger packs, as well as packs of deli meats and all the condiments you could imagine. While I looked at all the groceries that had been stored for us, I couldn't help thinking, *At least with me doing the cooking, I won't piss Todd off.* For that reason alone, I was glad to cook. I began to brown two packs of hamburger, using a large iron skillet I found in a drawer under the stove.

When Mike and Yeoman came into the kitchen, Yeoman said, "You only used two packs of hamburger? You should probably cook at least three or even four packs. I love tacos, and I'm starving."

Mike just laughed as he opened the fridge and got out two more packs of hamburger meat.

Soon, the tacos were ready with all the fixings, which included diced tomatoes, grated cheese, shredded lettuce, sliced jalapeños, refried beans, taco sauce, and ranch dressing. We sat around the big wooden kitchen table and ate the best tacos I had ever cooked. I was almost as hungry as Yeoman, or maybe it was the cold beer added to the hot tacos. Whatever the reason, I ate at least four tacos and drank three cold Coronas before I said, "Enough. I'll clean up the kitchen while you guys finish eating."

After the kitchen was cleaned up, the three of us retreated

to the front porch with beers in hand and found comfortable rocking chairs to enjoy the evening.

Mike spoke first. "I heard a shot about ten this morning from the direction Brian was hunting. I guess he was right when he said he'd be the first to kill a big gobbler."

Yeoman then said, "Too bad we can't get a cell signal. I'm sure Brian has texted several pictures of his turkey to us and the guys back in Davie County."

As the evening dragged on, each of us told about our turkey-hunting experiences of the day. When I relayed the story about scaring every turkey in the woods away, it was funny even to me. Mike and Yeoman both heard and saw lots of turkeys during their first day of hunting but never got a shot.

Mike said, "I was competing against lots of hens to attract the gobblers' attention."

Yeoman agreed. "Same here. I guess Brian just waited them out."

"What do you mean, waited them out?" I asked.

Mike said, "Remember, the hens go to the gobbler early in the morning. Then, after breeding, the hens slip off from the gobbler to lay their eggs. When all the hens are gone from the gobbler, he'll get lonely."

"When the gobbler's all alone, he'll be looking for a new girlfriend. That's when he's vulnerable to being called in by you," said Yeoman. "When he comes to you thinking you're his new lover, you shoot him right in the face."

Mike then added, "Yep, it's always the filly that gets a man in trouble."

"What are you talking about, Mike?" I asked.

"Well, it's true. When a buck goes into rut, he goes crazy chasing does and gets himself shot by a hunter," said Mike.

"A gobbler looking to get lucky with a hen gets shot right in the face. And when two men fight, you can bet it's because of a woman," said Yeoman.

"It's always the filly that gets turkeys, deer, men, and a lot of other male species' asses whooped," said Mike.

Yeoman and I both laughed and agreed with Mike's theory.

Yeoman stood up and said, "Boys, it's getting late, and four-thirty comes early. I'm going to fix me a couple of sandwiches, grab a couple of cookies, and turn in."

"Me, too, but I'm stuffed from all those tacos. See y'all in the morning," said Mike.

I got up from my rocking chair, said my good-nights, then retired into my bedroom. Once I was in bed, I checked my cell phone for the possibility of a signal, hoping I might be able to call Bonnie and wish her good night. But the screen said, "No service," and soon I drifted off to sleep.

168

CHAPTER ELEVEN

The next morning, I woke to the smell of frying bacon and the noise of banging frying pans. I quickly got up and rushed to the restroom to get rid of all those beers I had the night before. I returned to the bedroom and put on my turkey clothes and boots.

When I walked into the kitchen, Yeoman said, "Sleeping in today, are you?"

I looked at the clock on the kitchen wall and was shocked to see it was only four A.M. "I thought we were getting up at four-thirty, Yeoman," I said.

"Since you cooked supper last night, Yeoman and I

decided to cook breakfast. But you can clean up the mess," said Mike.

"Thanks, guys. That's what I do every day back home," I added.

"Yeah, right," Mike replied.

After breakfast, we got in our Rangers and headed up our mountains as dawn began to break. I parked my Ranger in the same spot as the morning before and found my way into the woods. I sat at the same tree as the morning before. When the woods came alive and the songbirds began to welcome me into their world, I couldn't help giggling, thinking how that gobbler had scared the crap out of me the morning before. I kept hoping for a gobbler to gobble on his own that morning. I dreaded to blow that dang owl call or crow call.

When daylight finally came and songbirds lit up the morning, there were no gobbles on my mountain. I had no choice but to try to shock-gobble a tom turkey using a crow call. I took the Knight and Hale crow call out of my hunting vest and blew into it. I anticipated the *Caw* sound of a crow, but instead it sounded like a sick chicken rooster. Not one gobbler answered. I hadn't even heard a hen yelp that morning. I thought it was going to be a long day, since I scared every turkey off my mountain yesterday.

When the morning turned to midday, I decided that while I was on that beautiful mountain, I should explore what God had created. I thought, *Who knows, maybe I can find some morel mushrooms.* Morels were better known in my neck of the woods as "dry-land fish." Morels look like small Christmas trees. They have a brown honeycomb appearance, with pits making up their caps or tops. Morels grow in the woods, usually around the base of poplar trees or dying elms. Some folks say that in the mountains of North Carolina, you can find morels in old, dying apple orchards. The best way to eat morels is to fry them just like fish, simply by rolling them in flour and cornmeal and frying them in a cast-iron skillet with your favorite oil. Once fried, morels taste just like fried fish and are considered a delicacy, especially in the South.

I got up from my hunting spot and walked slowly down the mountain toward a slow-moving stream. At the base of the mountain were lots of poplar trees, where I began my search for the tasty mushrooms. It didn't take long before I found my first morel growing at the base of a big, old poplar.

It was almost covered by last fall's leaves and was well hidden. I was very careful to pinch off the mushroom at its base so I would not kill the scrumptious treat. Even though I knew I would never return to that spot, it was good to leave the base for other hunters to gather. I forgot all about turkey hunting and continued to find lots of morels throughout the rest of the day.

As the day turned to evening, I gathered my morels and headed back to the Ranger and began the short ride to the camp. While I rode, I began thinking that, if I concentrated more on hunting and less on exploring, I might kill my first turkey tomorrow.

As I approached the base camp, I saw Yeoman standing in the backyard unloading his Ranger. I pulled my vehicle right beside his and asked, "Any luck today, my friend?"

Yeoman said, "I heard several gobblers this morning on roost, but when they flew down they quit gobbling. I soft-called all day, and a few gobbled. I guess they had hens with them and weren't interested in me."

"Well, I didn't hear or see a thing, with the exception of several big patches of dry-land fish," I said.

Yeoman said, "I didn't even think to look for morels. How many did you find?"

"I got over four dozen in this sack, more than enough for our supper," I said.

Yeoman responded, "Yep, enough for you and me. I think Mike killed a turkey this morning and won't be joining us for supper. I heard a shot around seven-thirty this morning."

"Good for Mike," I said. "Now, let's get to frying us some dry-land fish and maybe some fried potatoes with onions for supper."

"We're going to have coleslaw and baked beans with hushpuppies, too, aren't we?" Yeoman added with concern.

I laughed and said, "Sure, if you'll do the dishes and clean up the kitchen."

Yeoman said, "Deal," as he gathered his gear and headed into the cabin. The old screen door slammed behind him, and he yelled back at me, "Hurry up, Rumsey, I'm hungry!"

It wasn't long until the whole house smelled like fish frying, not to mention cooked onions and potatoes. I ate at least a dozen mushrooms, and Yeoman finished the rest, along with all the fixings. Afterward, I got up from the table and said, "You know, I was only kidding about you cleaning up by yourself."

"Yeah, I know. Let's hurry up and get out on the front porch and have a cold beer," Yeoman said.

After about three beers, I said, "Yeoman, I didn't see or hear any turkeys today. I think I scared all of them to the other mountains. Brian and Mike each killed a turkey, and you heard and saw turkeys today, but me, nothing."

"So what's your point, Rumsey?" said my friend.

"I think I'm going to hunt on Brian's mountain tomorrow," I said. "Brian killed his turkey the day before yesterday, and I'm sure that the turkeys remaining on his mountain have settled down and are huntable."

"Hey, you and I both know the rules John set," said Yeoman. "You can hunt only the mountain you were assigned to."

"John ain't here and, besides, we ain't never coming back this way again," I said. "The hell with John, his crazy boy, and their rules."

"Man, you must be missing Bonnie bad," said Yeoman. "I don't think I've ever seen you this fired up."

"Yep, I sure do miss Bonnie, but that's not it," I answered. "I want every chance to kill a Virginia gobbler. Hell, all I hunted today were those darn mushrooms."

"Well, then, hunting Brian's mountain will probably be your best chance to kill a turkey, Jack. John will never know," Yeoman said.

I passed Yeoman another beer when I got up from my rocker and opened the front door.

"Good night, my friend. See you at four-thirty," Yeoman said.

THE TURKEY KILLER: A Novel by JACK SNOW

CHAPTER TWELVE

The next morning, I was awakened by the smell of coffee and frying bacon and the sound of Yeoman singing "You Are My Sunshine." When I got to the kitchen, I asked him, "What did you do with that money I gave you, Yeoman?"

Yeoman said, "What money?"

Smiling, I said, "For singing lessons. I'd just as soon hear my dog bark."

Yeoman burst out laughing and said, "I guess it really was pretty bad."

After a great breakfast of pancakes and bacon, Yeoman

and I loaded our Rangers for our last day of turkey hunting. This time, I thought I would have a better chance of killing a gobbler because I was headed up the mountain where Brian got his turkey. Excited, I fired up the Ranger and followed the sign up the road to mountain #1. Soon, I reached the top. Just like on the mountain where I had hunted, there was a parking place for the Ranger. I parked and gathered my hunting vest and headed into the dark woods, hoping today would mark my first turkey kill.

I set up by a big white oak about three hundred yards into the forest. Soon, owls began their morning hooting ritual, and I must have heard at least six gobblers sounding off while on roost. I was so excited, thinking I had made the right decision to hunt on Brian's assigned mountain. I had gobblers in front of me and to my right. They were even gobbling at each other.

It wasn't long before the turkeys flew off their roosting spots and landed on the ground, looking for hens. Directly in front of me, I saw a huge gobbler approximately a hundred yards away. He was not gobbling but was strutting like he was the boss stud on the mountain. He appeared to be bigger than a fifty-gallon drum. I was so excited! I hoped he couldn't hear my heart beating in my chest.

Now was the time for action. I quickly reached into my vest and retrieved my Knight and Hale friction call and striker. I was shaking when I pulled the tip of the striker across the top half of the call, making the sweetest hen call ever. My stud gobbler in front of me went crazy and gobbled three or four times in a row. *He's coming*, I thought. I laid down the call, picked up my gun, and got ready for the kill. There was no need to call, since the gobbler was coming straight for me, strutting and gobbling every few steps. He came at me fast, and I was ready to pull the trigger when he got within forty yards. It must have been only a minute or so before he got within range for the kill. I took close aim at the gobbler's huge white head and slowly pulled the trigger. The gun erupted in a loud boom. The gobbler fell over, then jumped high into the air and landed back on the ground, all the while flopping like crazy. My severely wounded trophy somehow managed to limp over the top of a nearby hill.

After things settled down, I slipped through the woods to where I had shot the gobbler. It didn't take long for me to find enough blood and feathers to know my gobbler was hurt and dying. I looked in the direction the gobbler had run and knew that, just as with a hurt deer, I must not rush the retrieve. It was important to let the bird die quietly. Moving too quickly would just push my big gobbler farther into the woods.

After about thirty minutes, I couldn't wait any longer. With shotgun in hand, I began slowly walking through the woods in the direction my gobbler ran. I had gone only a few yards when I saw my bird face down with his wings spread outward. He looked huge, and I couldn't wait to get my hands on my first turkey kill. When I reached him, I saw that I had killed a very old bird. He had spurs an inch and a half long and what I estimated to be a twelve-inch beard.

Even though there was no cell signal, I retrieved my phone and began taking pictures of my first turkey and the surrounding woods. I sure didn't want to ever forget this moment. When I began to scan the side of the mountain, recording a video, I saw what appeared to be a large pool of blood only twenty yards farther up the mountain. I thought, *How strange. Must have been a bear or coyote that killed a deer or fawn and devoured it there.* Slowly and cautiously, I approached the blood pool, still recording my video. Then I saw there was no fur from a deer. I plainly saw that whatever had been killed was dragged down the side of the mountain toward a big thicket at the bottom. With my gobbler secured over my shoulder and my shotgun in hand, I slowly followed the blood trail toward the thicket. When I reached the bottom of the hill, I laid my gobbler on the ground and moved ever so cautiously into the brush, still following the blood trail.

When it ended, I couldn't help screaming at the sight of my friend Brian lying in a huge pool of dried blood. I knew immediately that he was dead from a shotgun blast to his chest. His entire body was covered in blood, dirt, leaves, and flies. I started to run as fast as I could up the mountain toward where my Ranger was parked. It seemed like it took me hours to reach the Polaris. I was completely exhausted and so badly scared I was shaking uncontrollably.

With my gun in hand, and ready for an attack, I sat in the Ranger trying to calm down and think about an escape plan and about getting to Yeoman. I thought, *Who could have killed Brian, one of my best friends? Maybe some hunter crossed over the mountain from the national game land and shot Brian by accident. Maybe there was a killer in these mountains. Maybe John or his half-crazy son, Todd, finally went off the deep end.* All I knew was that I needed to protect myself and get Yeoman and find help from the main lodge.

I drove my Ranger as fast as I could up the mountain where Yeoman was hunting. When I got to the top and reached the designated parking area, I saw no sign of Yeoman or his Ranger. I thought, *A big man like Yeoman wouldn't walk far from his UTV.* I also thought, *Yeoman could have decided to hunt on Mike's mountain, or he could have killed a gobbler and was back at the lodge, or he could have been killed and was somewhere in these mountains.* I needed to reach the lodge to get help, but first I had to check Mike's mountain in case Yeoman was hunting there.

I turned my Ranger around as quickly as possible and headed straight for Mike's hunting area. I drove as fast as I could toward the parking area on top of Mike's mountain. When I got close, I saw a Ranger in the designated spot. I jumped out of my vehicle and ran toward the parked

Ranger. I saw what appeared to be a lot of blood that had run down the side bed of the vehicle and dried there. Fear was running through every vein of my body as I approached the Ranger, expecting to find Yeoman dying there.

In the back of the Ranger, I found my buddy Mike and quickly saw that he, too, had been shot in the chest and was dead. I was half crazed with fear and dread of who else I would find shot.

There was nothing I could do but save myself and get to the lodge to call the authorities for help. I drove down the mountain past the base camp and headed down the dusty road toward the lodge. I was thinking crazy thoughts like, *Now I know why John insisted we hunt the exact mountains he chose. That made it easier to find which hunter he or his crazy son wanted to kill, and in what order.*

When I got closer to the lodge, I saw Todd running through a grassy field, headed in my direction. Todd had a wild, almost crazed look on his face. I saw a shotgun in his hands, and his clothes were covered in blood. I slid the Ranger to a stop in the middle of the dirt road and yelled for Todd to stop. He didn't pay any attention but continued running toward me, trying to scream while holding tight to his turkey gun. I had to make the biggest decision of my life. I slowly raised my shotgun and again demanded that Todd stop. Even with my gun raised, Todd continued running toward me while making loud, crazy sounds, as if he were trying to tell me I might be his next victim. I don't remember when I pulled the trigger. I only remember the sound when my turkey gun exploded and I saw Todd fall in his tracks. Todd hit the ground hard and began wailing and rolling around. I jumped from the Ranger and ran to his side. I grabbed his gun and threw it far away from Todd and myself. I saw that I had shot him in both legs, and that he needed medical help quickly or he might bleed to death.

I got back into the Ranger, drove quickly to the front yard of the lodge, and stopped at the porch steps. I grabbed my cell phone and called 911. I relayed to the operator the address and told her there was a wounded man who needed help immediately. I cried hysterically when I told her about my dead friends I had left on top of the mountains.

While I was on the phone with the 911 operator, the front door of the lodge slowly opened, and there stood

Yeoman. "What the hell is going on?" he asked. "I was in the kitchen fixing me a sandwich, and I heard a gunshot that came from the front yard."

I yelled back, "Yeoman, get in the truck! We got to get out of here now!"

With a puzzled look, Yeoman said, "What's the rush? I was beginning to eat my lunch." Yeoman started to speak again but stopped. He had a strange look on his face. Without speaking another word, my friend Yeoman bowed his chest out with his shoulders back and fell face forward onto the front porch. When Yeoman's big body hit the floor, I plainly saw a large butcher knife stuck into his back between his shoulder blades.

Directly behind him stood my old friend Blaine, holding another bloody knife in his hand. Blaine had a crazed, wild look on his face while he stared into my eyes. Blaine was dressed in full camo and looked like he had just stepped out of the jungles of Vietnam. I quickly raised my gun, aiming directly toward Blaine's chest.

Blaine just stared at me with a crazy smile and said, "See, Jack, I told you man was the hardest animal to kill. I've hunted y'all for the last couple of days, just like I hunted in Vietnam. Brian and Mike didn't have a clue in the world that while they were hunting turkeys, I was hunting them. I hunted each of them as I would have hunted a turkey or a wild animal, just as I hunted many men years ago. While I hunted Brian and Mike, I crowed like a crow, called like an owl, and gobbled just like a turkey to fool your friends." Blaine laughed loudly. "They actually thought I was that big gobbler they were just about to kill. I was so cunning that I didn't reveal myself to Brian or Mike until the very last moment of their lives. I was excited to see the fear in their eyes the moment they realized I was their big gobbler and they were about to die.

"After I watched each of your friends slowly die, I came back to the lodge and put a huge butcher knife into John's chest while his son, Todd, watched and cried," said Blaine. "When John fell to the floor, Todd ran from the house, and I watched through the window when you shot Todd and left him to die. I thought about sparing Yeoman's life until I saw you and him at camp last night eating supper. I realized that if I didn't kill Yeoman, he would blame you for his friends getting murdered, for it was you who talked those guys into coming to Texas and finally to their last hunt and death here in Virginia. So, you see, Jack, I'm still looking after you the same as I did when we were together in Mexico the first time we met. I wanted you to watch your best friends killed, the same as I watched my friends and fellow soldiers draw their last breaths in Vietnam. Now, you know exactly what I lived with all these years."

Then, with a smile on his face, Blaine said, "Now, my friend, either I'm going to kill you or you will kill me. Either way, one of us will breathe our last breath today."

Blaine jumped from the porch with the bloody butcher knife and screamed as he ran in my direction. I watched as the blast from my shotgun hit him square in the chest and knocked him back onto the porch. Blaine died a violent death but was finally free from all his demons.

I ran past Blaine, hoping I might be able to save Yeoman. Once I got to Yeoman's side, it was plain to see my friend was dead. I looked into the lodge and saw John lying on the bedroom floor in a pool of blood from a knife wound to his chest.

Though it seemed like hours, it was only minutes until I heard the sheriff's siren racing toward the lodge. Shortly, a medical helicopter arrived and picked up Todd and took him to the trauma center in Roanoke.

EPILOGUE

"Cannon, the next two days were just a blur, with all the questions from the sheriff's office and going back onto the mountains to retrieve my closest friends' bodies," I said. "On the third day, I got into Mike's truck and drove home to Davie County and my lovely Bonnie. It wasn't long after my friends were buried that Bonnie and I realized we just couldn't live in peace on our little farm anymore. The memories of my dear friends and their tragic deaths were more than I could bear. We soon sold our farm and moved here close to Boone to live out the rest of our days in whatever peace comes our way. That is, until you stepped into our world."

With that, the short, pudgy young man rose from his chair and, with tears running down his face, hugged me tightly. Cannon then looked into my eyes and said, "Thank you for telling me the story of my grandpa. I promise I will not bother you or Miss Bonnie again."

I watched Cannon drive slowly down the dirt road toward the main highway and back into his world. In some ways, I think my old friend Yeoman came to visit one last time that day.

ACKNOWLEDGMENTS

Tremendous thanks go out to some of the most important people in my life.

To my sweet daughter, Jennifer, who tried to help me with spelling and story content, even though I didn't listen.

To Brian McDaniel, my close friend and a really great guy. Brian and I have had lots of fun hunting and fishing together throughout the years. Brian is always there to lend a helping hand around my farm and is much appreciated by me and my neighbors.

To one of my closest friends, Mike Wall, who, while we were traveling on business, always encouraged me to write. Mike has long been one of my biggest supporters and continues to encourage me to do more.

To Blaine Friermood, who allowed me to make his character into an out-of-control friend who had lost all reality. Blaine is a great friend and is nothing like the Blaine at the South Texas Hilton as described in this book.

To my close friends Harold Knight and David Hale, who allowed me to use their names and mention their fine products throughout the book. Also, I want to thank Harold and David for letting me hunt with them the last fifteen years on opening day of turkey season. Both are legends in the hunting industry.

To various friends and neighbors who participated in many hunting trips and cookouts at my shed.

To my late father, Fred Snow, who gave me the gifts of gab and storytelling. Dad had only an eighth-grade education but was one of the smartest and kindest men I have ever known.

AUTHOR'S AFTERWORD

For many years, *The Turkey Killer* was just an idea. When I began this book, I wrote it in bits and pieces. Sometimes, I would go almost a year and never think about writing or finishing it. For twenty-seven years, I traveled all over the United States and talked to large and small companies, trying to secure their business. Through all those travels, when I addressed those customers, I usually had a story or a joke to tell. I told stories in an effort to get potential customers to at least remember my name. As mentioned in the acknowledgments, my father taught me so much about people, life, and my responsibility to be as good a person as possible. But two of the most important things Dad gave me were the gift of gab and a wild imagination.

I retired April 1, 2019. Soon afterward, I found myself looking for something productive to do around our small farm. I helped Bonnie get the house in order, cleaned every single inch of my shed, and caught every fish in my pond. After running out of chores, I felt it was a good time to finish *The Turkey Killer.*

The idea for this story came to life while I was in the mountains of Virginia. It was early in my turkey-hunting career, and I found myself all alone on top of a mountain, trying to figure out how to call a turkey within range of my Remington gun. I really had no idea what I was doing. I was bored, and my imagination ran wild. What if a serial killer were on the mountain with me? What if, while I was hunting turkeys, a serial killer was hunting me, using all the turkey-hunting tactics that I was trying to use? Just like that, *The Turkey Killer* began to take shape.

I hope you have enjoyed *The Turkey Killer.*

www.ingramcontent.com/pod-product-compliance
Lightning Source LLC
Chambersburg PA
CBHW030757190726

48285CB00003B/899